# CONVINCING DERRICK

## A SWEET ROMANTIC SUSPENSE

### SARA BLACKARD

Want to know how it all began? Find out what propelled Zeke and the team to create the Stryker Security Force by signing up for Sara Blackard's newsletter, and you'll receive **Mission Out of Control**, the *Stryker Security Force* prequel for FREE.

www.sarablackard.com

# ONE

DERRICK NICHOLSON GRITTED his teeth as sweat ran down his spine. The Utah desert outside of Moab was the last place he wanted to be in the middle of summer, but he couldn't leave the abused to suffer another day. When he'd gotten the call from his friend saying there were two horses for him to rescue, he'd hitched up the trailer and jetted down the interstate, all geared up to play hero. Now, the rancid ammonia smell of the filthy barn battled with the nauseating sight of the beaten and starved horses, and he wasn't sure which one soured his stomach more. Would today be the day he snapped and the hero became the villain?

A set of dogs had barked incessantly from their kennels since he backed up to the corral a few minutes before, their frantic yips and skinny frames magnifying Derrick's agitation. He squeezed his hands around the slip-slop fencing of the corral, red sand and rough wood grinding into his palms. If he didn't grip tight, he might stomp over to the cocky man standing in front of the ranch-style house smoking a cigarette and pulling drinks from his beer like he was here to watch the show. The deputy standing next to Derrick, making sure the transfer of the horses happened without a hitch, might not take too kindly to Derrick's fist breaking the horses' owner's nose. Then again, with how white the lawmaker's knuckles were where he strangled the fence, he might let Derrick get a solid couple of punches in before pulling him off.

Derrick rolled his shoulders as he dragged his gaze away from the house and surveyed the ranch. The sun inched down toward the red-rocked mountains in the west, gathering darkness behind the derelict buildings. The taste of dirt and rotting hay lay thick on Derrick's tongue. He pulled his beat-up Stetson off his shaved head and wiped the sweat that ran into his eyes. He'd rather wait until the sun fully hid behind the horizon and cooler temperatures settled over the desert before he transported the poor horses, but he didn't trust himself to not follow through with the desire to pummel the man responsible for the animals' torture.

"What's happening with the dogs?" Derrick pointed his chin to the kennels as a dog yelped and limped the length of the fencing.

The deputy sighed and pushed his hat back. "The local animal control is coming over to get them."

"Since the jerk owner isn't rotting in jail, did he at least get fined?" Derrick couldn't hold back the disgust in his voice.

The deputy snorted a humorless laugh and shook his head. "The man got out of it. Claimed he inherited the animals from his pa who just passed, and the old man was the one who abused the animals." He stood up straight and crossed his arms over his chest. "Which is the truth, but since he's lived out here with his pa for the last five years, I have a hard time believing that dung heap."

So the dude would get off scot-free? Derrick's jaw hurt where his teeth squeezed together. He needed to get out of here in double time, otherwise he might find himself examining the inside of a jail cell.

"I'm going to open up the trailer and lead these poor things in." Derrick stomped to his truck to get his lariat. "Mind guiding me to the gate?"

"Nah, man." The deputy followed close. "I'll help however I can."

"Thanks. When I get close, swing the gate open and I'll back right into the opening."

Derrick jumped into his truck and backed the trailer up to the gate. Thankfully, the opening was just wide enough for the trailer to butt up against it. Once the ramp was down, the horses wouldn't be able to escape through gaps in the gate.

Derrick grabbed the halters and lead rope from the backseat of his truck and handed them to the deputy. "Just drape those over the fence for me, please."

After tossing his hat into the front seat, Derrick looped the coiled lariat through the strap he'd attached to his belt. If all went well, there would be no need for the rope. After the first heartbreaking rescue, where the horse had snapped her leg trying to get away from the loop Derrick had swung, he tried to approach the animals with as little intimidation as possible, which was hard for a six-foot-four man to accomplish. No hat, no loop swinging through the air—just him, a bucketful of tasty grains, and his calm, low voice crooning to them.

Derrick climbed over the fence and froze when the horses skittered away to the other side. He might just get his wish of transporting the horses in the cool of night. Though he much preferred the thrill of bull riding or the feel of a horse darting from the gate, the army had pounded patience into his essence. He pulled a bucket he already had filled with sweetened grain from where the saddles were usually stored at the back of the trailer. Inching forward with excruciating slowness, he gave the bucket a shake and spoke soft, sweet nothings to them.

The dark brown mare snorted, reaching her nose toward him. The palomino with gashes across her hindquarters shied away, hiding behind the brown. Derrick took another step forward, grabbing a handful of the molasses-covered grains and holding it out with his palm up.

"Come on, girls. Let's get you out of here." He cringed as he noticed a festering wound along the brown's shoulder. "So, what should we call you? Brownie?"

She blew a raspberry and shook her head, pulling him back to his childhood. She reminded him of his brother's horse. Chip had been a dark brown with a personality that matched Derrick's daredevil brother, Josiah. Derrick's heart twisted like it always did when he thought of Josiah. His brother's shocked expression as the rocks gave out from under him, tumbling him into the jagged ravine, filled Derrick's mind. He pushed the troubling memory aside, knowing the horses before him would sense any agitation in him.

"No? You don't like Brownie?" Derrick moved a step closer. "Yeah, that's not very original. How about Annie? You look like an Annie to me."

She stomped and huffed in irritation.

"I guess Annie is out." He chuckled and stretched his hand closer.

She lifted her nose, her nostrils flaring as she sniffed the air. She took a step toward him and hope jolted through his skin. He stuffed it down, knowing she could bolt with one wrong move from him. The palomino lifted her head above the other's back and whinnied a warning, her eyes wide. The brown snuffed an answer but stepped closer anyway.

"Come on, girl. I've got some nice, yummy grain waiting in the trailer for you, darling."

As she continued her approach, Derrick inched backward, closer to the trailer. He stopped halfway and let her catch up. She cautiously stretched her neck out and, with careful movements, lipped the grain out of his hand. A breeze blew the putrid smell of infected flesh to him. He swallowed the lump in his throat, clearing away the emotion clogging his voice.

"See. That wasn't so bad." He took a step back as he jiggled the bucket again.

She nickered softly and flicked her ears forward. Progress. Now, to get her and her friend into the trailer.

"Mind telling your partner I'm not so bad?" He stepped back as she stretched her neck out, causing her to walk toward him.

With a slow, steady pace, he worked the brown into the trailer, pouring some grain from the bucket into the feed box, and closing her in the front unit. A high-pitched neigh preceded the palomino as she darted into the trailer after her friend as if afraid she'd get left behind alone. Derrick chuckled as he gently closed the second unit and gave the golden horse her reward.

He shut the back doors with a satisfied sigh and turned to the deputy. "All right. I'm off."

The deputy gripped Derrick's hand in a firm shake. "Hope you can help those girls."

"Me, too." Derrick thought of the brown and her courage to come to him. "I think they'll be okay."

"Yeah." The deputy glanced to the house and scowled. "Drive safe, man."

Derrick saluted, gathered his gear from the fence, and stalked to the truck. The brown gave him hope—hope that he could save them. The longing to get a ranch of his own and turn this part-time venture into something more permanent itched under his skin.

His family at Stryker filled his mind. Who was he kidding? He could never leave his friends. He had a responsibility to them, one that overrode the desires of his heart.

# TWO

KIKI PAYNE'S coffee steamed next to her arm as she scanned her four computer screens. Her eyebrows furrowed, and she swiftly clicked through the options playing out before her, jotting them in her notebook.

"Okay," she said to her computer screens. "I think we're ready."

She rolled her shoulders, stretched her arms high above her head, and sat back in the chair. Wrapping her hands around her coffee mug, she stared out the window of her office. The sky above the mountains had lightened to dark blue, signaling that the early morning pinks and oranges would soon paint the heavens, and her starry friends would blink out until tomorrow. She loved this time of day, loved the hope that came with each rise of the sun over the Rocky Mountains.

Back home in Texas, she'd never noticed the sunrise. She'd been more busy with gathering every dollar that she could before heading out to find some fun. She hadn't understood how meaningless her life was until she found herself stripped of her family, living in Colorado with a bunch of strangers.

Closing her eyes, she breathed in the peppermint and orange oils misting from her diffuser. Now that she had lived on Zeke's ranch for over half a year, the image of family had solidified in her being. The ragtag group of friends at Stryker Security Force bound by love and life filled Kiki's head.

She smiled as she opened her eyes to the first pink lining the horizon. Odd that the only blood relation here was her niece, Evangeline, but Kiki couldn't deny that the men and women that lived on the massive ranch were more a family than she'd ever witnessed. While she still edged along the outskirts of the group, like the light rose color lining the sky, she desired nothing more than to pierce the invisible barrier that held her back and spread like the dawn into the depths of the family.

Maybe then the darkness her own kin created would flee like the night.

Kiki's throat ached from unshed tears, and she swallowed down the reminder of her parents' actions. She'd probably never overcome that taint, no matter how hard she tried. Honestly, she wouldn't blame Zeke and the others if they never fully trusted her. She certainly wouldn't.

"Enough of that." She spun to her computer.

She shook off the dreary thought, dipped a green apple slice into peanut butter, and crunched a bite off as she examined the stocks again. The crisp snap of apple and tangy taste focused her gloomy thoughts back to where they belonged. There wasn't much she did well that was worthwhile besides day trading. Shopping didn't really count, and her parents' actions had jerked her charity work from the table with everyone assuming she was knee-deep in corruption like her father. If she didn't hop to it, her trading plan for the day would slip past her, and she wouldn't even have that.

She glanced at her clock. 5:47 a.m. Good, she still had plenty of time before the market opened. She strategized until the stocks started jumping, then fell headlong into how she stayed anchored to reality. Thank goodness her father had done her a solid when she was fourteen and forced her to learn day trading. While not your typical father-daughter bonding activity, it was about the only helpful thing he'd done for her. While her approach to the career differed vastly from the great Kevin Payne, she made a decent income off of it.

Her phone dinged, and she pulled up the text message.

LENA: You gonna make it or did the computer swallow you whole?

Kiki smiled at her friend's reminder as she glanced at the clock, glad for the humor that the serious Lena showed more and more the longer she was there. 11:15 a.m. Kiki still had forty-five minutes to get to the training room at the old stables. She normally wasn't late, but Lena knew how Kiki could get caught up in her work.

KIKI: I'll be there as soon as I change.

LENA: Be late, and I'll make your day even more miserable than normal.

Kiki sat up straight. Lena most likely joked, but given that she was ex-military with a penchant for dealing out pain, Kiki didn't want to test her theory. She double-checked her stocks to make sure she hadn't missed anything, jotted down her numbers, and rushed out of her office to her bedroom across the hall.

When she'd first arrived, she'd lived in one of the bedrooms of the main house designated for clients. Then when Samantha, Eva's mom, had married Zeke, the owner of Stryker Security, Kiki had moved into the apartment over the garage with Lena Rebel, a new member of the Stryker team the guys had served with in the army, and Tina West, the nanny-turned-K-9-trainer. Yet when Rafe married his best friend's sister, Piper, people had shifted around again. She loved that about this group, how everyone would change things up to accommodate. So different from how her parents had taught her.

Kiki grabbed her workout skort she'd just purchased and the matching tank top from the dresser and quickly changed out of her jeans. Tying her gym shoes on, she dashed out her door and down the stairs, barely noticing the impressive ranch house.

She liked the new arrangement better than living in the apartment. Now, she shared the guest house with Lena, Tina, and Chloe, when she wasn't on tour. Derrick, Cooper, and Davis also shared the house, but with everyone but herself coming and going on Stryker assignments or concert tours, sometimes the enormous place could be empty as a tomb.

What used to be the Man Cave, as Rafe called it— though how a three-story, eight-bedroom luxury ranch house could be called such a thing blew her mind—now was the Pathetic Singles Pad. Again, Rafe's name. The others threw a fit every time he called it that, especially Chloe and Tina who were in solid relationships, so Kiki kept her agreement with him to herself. She probably would only call herself pathetic, though. No one else in the house deserved that moniker.

The women lived upstairs. The guys lived down, and

they all shared the main level in the middle. The house came complete with a fancy kitchen she didn't know how to operate, a pool table she could never hit balls on, and a home theater where she watched more westerns and action movies than she'd ever thought existed. As much as she was out of her element, she loved it.

The hot sunshine hit her skin, causing her to pause on the front porch. She breathed deeply the fresh, bright scent of warm grass and invigorating pine. She'd take the dry mountain air over the stifling humidity of Texas any day. She smiled, then bounced down the stairs, her steps lighter than before.

The whinnying of a horse drew her attention to the corral where two horses she hadn't seen before huddled in a corner. Her forehead furrowed at the ragged pair. Derrick must've saved another bunch.

Her heart picked up at the thought of the tall, dark, and completely off-limits man. She refused to ruin their friendship and make things awkward with everyone over her mountain-sized crush. She'd get over it, and, if not, she'd live. It wasn't like she had much of a heart left after her parents' betrayal.

Her phone chirped, and she swiped open the screen as she skipped down the stairs toward the training room. Her steps slowed and shoulders slumped. Her mother had sent another text.

MOM: Kiki, darling, are you ready to put this silliness aside and come home yet? We need to show a solid front for the vultures circling, and we can't do that with you off throwing a tantrum.

Kiki shouldn't feel guilty about her mother's distress. She really shouldn't. Her mom had also been in on Gregory's attempt to kidnap Eva last fall that had ended with Kiki bound and bloodied in the back of his car. She shuddered at the memory of overhearing her parents demand that her cousin get their granddaughter, no matter the cost.

Would they still demand the same, knowing what that cost would be?

Probably not.

Maybe.

She stopped and pushed her fingers over her eyelids. She honestly didn't know anymore. Almost every week she got a text from a so-called friend back home with the latest news article of the investigation into her parents' empire and a snide remark. Maybe it was time to get a new phone number.

Kiki questioned if she ever really knew her parents at all. How could she not have seen the magnitude of their shadiness? Was she really that naive?

She sniffed and blinked the moisture from her eyes. Well, whatever the case, she wasn't naive anymore. She had pushed her starry-eyed self off the cliff and down the mountain, replacing her with a stronger, more enlightened version of herself.

One that didn't bend to petulant demands.

She swiped the text message into the trash and shoved her phone into her skort pocket. If she wanted to be a new person, she needed to get to the training room and let Lena torture her. Being stronger meant more than just standing up to her parents. If she never wanted to be hurt like Gregory had hurt her again, she had to learn how to defend herself. Lena, warrior princess extraordinaire, was the perfect person to train up the old, weak Kiki into someone much improved.

# THREE

DERRICK STOOD in the shadows of the barn as he stared at Kiki with her head tipped back to the sun and a contented smile pushing her cheeks up. He'd watched her a lot since he carried her from Samantha's junker of a car last fall. Kiki's feet had been so bruised and cut she hadn't been able to walk for over a week. His lip twitched up on one side, remembering how much of a protest she'd raised every time he'd go to carry her somewhere. She hadn't wanted to put him or anyone else out. Still didn't.

The palomino whinnied from where she huddled behind the brown in the corral's corner. It had been a long night trying to coax that poor girl out of the trailer. She'd gotten the brown all riled up with her fussing, and now he was back to square one with them cowering from him. That was the way of rehabilitation—in both people and animals, probably. One step forward to healing, two or three steps back.

His gaze bounced from the horses to Kiki. She reminded him a lot of his horses. She'd come to them beat-up, heartbroken, and without a home. The times she'd come to the house with her cousin last fall trying to visit Eva, he'd sensed something different about her, like she hadn't been filled in on all the details of her family's mission.

When she'd done what she could to stop her psycho of a cousin from kidnapping Eva, she'd become one of the team, a part of the Stryker family. Convincing her of that had been a long, slow road he still wasn't sure they had finished traveling. The contented smile was a good sign. Much better than the forced one she often wore, like she wasn't sure if she was welcome in their merriment.

She pranced down the steps like a filly frolicking through the hayfield, her short skirt flapping in the wind. He stifled a laugh. Was she really going to work out with Lena in that getup? She looked like she was ready to go play tennis at some fancy health club, not improve her self-defense with Lena during their daily lessons.

The palomino whinnied loudly, like she was calling to Kiki for help. Kiki stopped, her eyes traveling over the corral and her forehead scrunching. He'd left so fast yesterday afternoon that he hadn't told her he was getting more horses, not that he had to check in or anything. Most of the time she steered clear of the barn, like she was afraid of the horses or something. Yet she always asked how things were going. Always kept tabs on which horses he brought in and how they were progressing.

She pulled her phone out of some pocket hidden in her skirt, though how one had hidden in the outfit was beyond him. The happy lift of her shoulders slumped, causing Derrick's muscles to tighten. She often received texts that would settle an invisible weight upon her slender shoulders. He couldn't imagine the pressure pushing from the heavy load after so many messages.

She never said anything. Never railed against whoever sent them or threw a fit. She'd tuck her phone away and paste on her million-dollar smile like everything was okay.

He had happened to be next to her phone when it had sounded an alert. The message that had popped up on the locked screen had his blood boiling. He'd asked her who sent it. She just shrugged and mumbled her friends back home and efficiently changed the subject. He wanted to take her phone and throw it in the manure heap. She didn't need that kind of stress, no matter who it came from.

If they couldn't see that Kiki differed from her conniving family, then they didn't deserve her devotion—didn't deserve her forgiveness. He scoffed and kicked a clod of dirt at his foot. He was so full of it, he sickened himself. If she wanted to forgive the petty ladder climbers and her sleazy relatives, who was he to judge?

No one, that's who.

Especially after his family had forgiven him for the unforgiveable. He held the blame for Josiah's death. If Derrick hadn't been trying to show off for his older brother while free climbing, Josiah wouldn't have had to rescue Derrick when fear froze him on that mountain's rock face. If Derrick had double checked their climbing gear like he was supposed to, he would have seen the broken spring-loaded cam and thrown it away instead of setting it in the crevice. Because of Derrick, that faulty cam had buckled under Josiah's heavier weight.

The guys razzed Derrick about how he always bugged them about their stuff. The nickname Mother Goose, or Goose for short, had been an unfortunate side effect of him clucking at them to triple check their gear. What most of them didn't know was his burning need for everything and everyone to be in order came from his colossal screw-up.

He had to do things right, to be perfect. He couldn't live with himself if he didn't do his best to always be prepared. So he made sure his team stayed safe, made sure he was always ready for any situation. Yet it was starting to wear on him. He wanted a slower pace, to not always have to be on guard.

He reached to scratch his lower back but stopped himself. The silicone scars he put on every morning to conceal his emergency escape tools itched under his clothes. Would he ever relax enough to go without the razor blades and handcuff keys he hid on his body every day?

Okay, maybe he took things a little too far. Since getting out of the army, the likelihood of capture had diminished to almost nil. That didn't keep him from preparing for the worst every morning. The hidden tools on his body and sewn into his clothing calmed him, gave him a sense of control.

He rubbed his hand on his neck to wipe away his discomfort.

He stepped out of the shadows as Kiki resumed her walk to the training center. Her eyes widened, then relaxed as a smile stretched across her face. His chest expanded, and he took a deep breath. *Calm down, man.* It wasn't him making joy beam from her that loosened his muscles. He hoped his presence brought all his friends a sense of relief, of camaraderie.

She'd become a close friend since she'd moved in, and most of the guys now spent more time with their wives and fiancées than with their bros. He got that. It was the next step of life he was glad they had taken. It just meant that he spent most of his off time with his housemates, and since Kiki wasn't ever off on assignments, when he stayed behind, they hung out. As friends. Nothing more.

Her startling blue eyes sparkled at him as she waved and picked up her pace to the corral fence. His heart kicked into overdrive, but he ignored it.

He wasn't going there with her.

She was just getting settled into life here and enjoyed being around Eva, while he got more anxious to leave the fast-paced life of playing bodyguard behind and get back to his cowboy roots. She deserved to be here with family after all she'd been through. So while Kiki, with her blue eyes the color of a clear Coloradan sky and her cheery disposition that made him smile, may get his heart riled like a bucking bronc, there really wasn't any reason to pursue a relationship beyond friendship.

"Hey, D. Looks like you got some new recruits." Kiki rested her arms on the top rail, her short stature barely allowing her shoulders to clear the bar.

"Yeah." Derrick leaned his side on the fence next to her. "I found these two darlings over in Utah. Got them here late last night."

She clicked her tongue. "Hey there, sweeties." Her soft voice had the mares standing their ears to attention. "You've come to a good place, little darlings. Derrick here is just about the nicest man you'll ever meet." Her neck pinked as she peeked over at Derrick and back to the horses. "Before you know it, you'll be out helping others heal."

The brown snickered and blew her lips at Kiki. She chuckled low, covering her mouth like she wanted to hold in her laughter. Heat bloomed through Derrick's chest and his hands broke out in a sweat. Okay, wow. He might not be as unaffected by Kiki as he thought. He straightened from the fence and casually wiped his hands on his jeans.

"I'm not sure if she's agreeing with me or doing the horse's equivalent of sticking her tongue out." Laughter bubbled through Kiki's words, causing an odd feeling to effervesce in Derrick's gut. Her smile wavered as she glanced up at him. "Well, I don't want to be late meeting Lena. Her torture is more intense than normal when I am."

Derrick grunted, unable to conjure words through the haze her laughter caused.

She gave him a slight, closed-mouth smile that didn't reach her suddenly sad eyes and waved as she headed off. Shoot. What the heck was wrong with him? *Come on, Nicholson, don't make things harder on her than it already is.*

"Kiki?" He forced through his tight throat.

"Yeah?" She turned, her hands wringing in front of her.

"I'm working them later if you want to stop by after you're done with Lena." Derrick pointed his chin to the horses. "I think it'd be good for them if you visit. Let them experience a softer, more gentle human than the jerks who owned them."

"You want me to help with them?" The shock in her voice made him regret not asking her before.

"Yeah. If you want, that is." Derrick pressed his lips together so he wouldn't say anything to make her doubt.

She glanced to the mares, her eyes softening as she stared. "Okay. I'm not sure how I can help, but I'll come by when I'm done."

"Good." Derrick stepped back toward the safety of the barn. "See you then."

She absentmindedly nodded as she headed toward the training room. He had a good hour to pull himself together and get his overactive mind under control. It might take a dunking in the trough, but for his friendship with Kiki, he'd do it. He didn't want to make it even harder to leave if he decided to start a ranch somewhere. He was positive the grime and frustration that came with working the battered animals would help him remember what was important—staying focused and figuring out what his next step was going to be. He couldn't do that with his mind tangled with Kiki's sweet smile and melodic laughter.

# FOUR

KIKI RUSHED toward the training center that used to be the stables before Zeke bought the ranch. It was funny how they completely remodeled the gigantic stable, with its indoor arena, into a shooting range, workout and training room, sick bay, lounge, and storage, and now there were horses on the property that had to be housed in the smaller barn by their place.

Of course, Derrick's side hustle came after the guys had been saving people's lives and taking down names, or whatever it was they did in the hero business. Not that it really was a hustle. He didn't make any money off rescuing the poor horses. When she'd asked why he did it, he'd just shrugged and said he needed more action than what the job brought.

The way her housemates talked, their bodyguard jobs more often left them bored than pumping their blood with the rush of adrenaline. Yet she'd seen the charred lawn last fall when Tina's car blew up and had bitten her nails down to the quick those days Jake and Chloe had crash landed in the middle of a blizzard and couldn't be rescued. She'd take the ribbing that came from the others about being a desk jockey any day if it meant she didn't have to deal with psycho stalkers and car bombs.

She was a wuss, and her friends all knew it. It was why Lena put Kiki through an hour of misery every day she could, to turn Kiki from the cream puff she was to something stronger. She didn't think she'd ever get past the pastry level, though maybe she'd make it to bear claw or apple fritter status. Those had more substance than a cream puff.

Geez, she must be hungry.

She glanced at her watch. Three minutes until the hour of agony began. Not enough time to grab anything from the lounge's fridge. She groaned and pushed her hand against her protesting stomach. Why hadn't she thought to eat before? She'd be starving by the time she finished getting pummeled.

The ragged mares in the corral, with their bones that stuck out beneath their skin, flashed in her brain. She shook her head. She was such a pampered whiner. She didn't know what it was like to starve. She had no clue what true suffering felt like. What she'd gone through since last fall was nothing compared to what others endured. She went from one place of privilege to another, with the barest hiccup in between.

Yep. Cream puff.

She pulled open the door to the training center and squared her shoulders, determined to ignore her hunger and give this training everything she had. She might never be a lean, mean fighting machine like Lena Rebel, but Kiki could train to counterattack before she ran away in fear, most likely screaming her head off.

Or crying.

She could see herself bawling if she ever got attacked. That's why she needed Lena's help. She couldn't live with a band of warriors and be the weak link. Not anymore. If she wanted to truly be a part of this hodgepodge family, then she had to toughen up and slough off the spoiled rich girl persona.

She followed the sound of voices and skin hitting skin to the training room. It looked like any other gym she'd ever been to, with workout equipment lining one wall and a bank of mirrors on the other. The only difference was the large mat in the center of the room that hadn't graced the upscale hangouts she'd been to back in Texas. That was where the real action happened.

Kiki stepped into the room, her eyes widening as Rafe and Lena circled each other in the middle of the mat. Rafe's face bled from a cut above his eyebrow, and Lena's jaw appeared reddened. Kiki backed up against the doorjamb, trying not to let the show upset her. She'd witnessed sparring since she moved here, but it still left her queasy, like the action movies she endured.

She'd never liked violence. She had even covered her eyes through cartoons growing up. Her brother and cousin Gregory had loved picking on her for it, torturing insects and small animals just to make her cry. So she'd pretended she had gotten over it, though inside, her gut had twisted with just the thought of violence.

Still did.

Which was why she avoided these sparring matches as much as she could and read sappy romances on her phone while the others enjoyed their movies. She didn't want to not be around everyone else. She enjoyed the way they critiqued the action films, often laughing at how unrealistic they were. She figured the sappier the romance of her book, the more it countered the movie. Give her a good rom-com any day.

Rafe swung his arm toward Lena's face. Kiki cringed as Lena ducked and laughed. A fist flew toward her face, and Lena laughed? Kiki shook her head. She'd never understand that.

"Oh, Malone, you've gone soft. Never figured marriage would turn you into a butterball," Lena taunted.

With his bulging biceps and shoulders that strained against his t-shirt, Rafe didn't look soft to Kiki. None of the guys with Stryker Security Force did.

"Soft? Rebel, you need to get out more if you think I've gone soft." Rafe faked a move left, but punched Lena hard in the gut when she countered.

Kiki fisted her hands at her side so she didn't cover her eyes. Lena barely grunted before she darted in close to Rafe, jabbed him twice in the belly, then landed one on his cheek before bounding back out of reach. One dark eyebrow rose on Lena's gorgeous face, and she smirked as she bounced on her toes.

As much as Kiki hated conflict, she envied Lena's strength. Would Kiki ever come close to what Lena could do? Probably not.

"Dang, Lena. Watch the face!" Rafe's smile contradicted his words. "You don't want to mess up perfection."

Lena snorted, her hands dropping from their guard. Rafe used the moment to attack, stepping quickly toward her. Kiki watched in awe and horror as Lena stepped into Rafe's advance instead of away. Her arm swung up, connecting with Rafe's chin. He dropped like a rag doll. The flopping sound of him hitting the mat rolled Kiki's stomach.

Kiki rushed forward when he didn't move. "Oh, no. What should we do?"

She knelt next to him, afraid to touch him and hurt him more. His chest moved as he breathed, but, other than that, he stayed completely still. Why wasn't Lena doing anything? Wasn't she some super combat medic or something?

"Lena? Help!" Kiki glanced up at her friend, blinking the sting from her eyes.

"Don't worry. He'll come around." Lena toed his leg. "I just knocked him out is all."

"But ..."

Kiki had seen the way his head had snapped. Her stomach clenched, and she was suddenly glad she'd forgotten to eat. Rafe groaned, and Kiki sat back in relief, brushing the tear that escaped down her cheek.

"See. You have to toughen up." Lena rolled her neck and pointed her chin at Kiki. "Can't neutralize a larger enemy if you aren't willing to use all your skills."

"But, Rafe isn't the enemy."

"If you don't train like your life depends on it, you will never succeed when a real enemy attacks. Is that what you want, Cookie?"

Kiki shook her head, a heaviness settling on her slumped shoulders. When Lena had first started calling Kiki Cookie, she'd said it was because Kiki was too darn sweet. Now, she wondered if it had more to do with her being weak rather than nice. She sniffed and placed her hand on Rafe's shoulder. There wasn't anything wrong with being sweet, though she longed to not be thought of as weak. She'd have to work on that more. Maybe watch the beat-em-up movies instead of burying her head in her book.

Rafe rolled over on to his back. His eyebrows furrowed

as his gaze landed on Kiki, then glared when they connected with Lena. He pushed up to sitting with a moan.

"You did the move on me, didn't you?" Rafe lifted an eyebrow as he rubbed his chin.

Lena shrugged. "You deserved it."

"Move? What move?" Kiki bunched her hands in her skort to keep from patting Rafe on the back in comfort, remembering how Lena had kicked the man while he was down.

Okay, that wasn't fair. She'd just nudged him.

"Sam taught us all this move she learned in Kajukenbo." Lena walked to her water bottle against the wall and took a deep drink.

"Kaju-yaya? What the heck is that?" Kiki rubbed her hand down her face. She really was clueless with this kind of stuff.

"Kajukenbo is a martial art from Hawaii. Sam's a black belt and taught us this move after she flattened Zeke." Rafe pressed the heel of his hand over his eye, then peeked from the other at her. His head had to be throbbing. "I haven't shown you that security feed yet?"

Kiki shook her head. She'd remember if she'd seen the graceful Samantha Greene take her tough husband out.

Rafe laughed, then quieted to a moan. "It's a good one. I'll show you later."

He pushed to his knees, shook his head, then stood up with a slight wobble. Would he be okay? Kiki scrambled to her feet, prepared to catch him if he fell again.

"Right now, I'm going home." He moved his head from side to side and winced. "Maybe if I whine to Piper, I'll get some sympathy."

Lena snorted. "One look at you, and Piper will go all

Florence Nightingale on you." She tipped her water bottle toward Rafe. "You can thank me later."

"With this killer headache, I don't think I'll be thanking you at all." Rafe lifted his hand as he headed for the door. "Good match."

"Any time you want a good thrashing, you know where to find me," Lena hollered after him.

"Whatever," Rafe scoffed. "I could take you."

Lena chuckled, took another drink, then inspected Kiki like she contemplated how to decimate her next victim. "What are you wearing?"

Kiki glanced down at the matching skort set. What could Lena possibly find wrong with it? So what if it was cute? It happened to also be functional.

"What?" Kiki lifted her hands in confusion.

"Nothing." Lena rolled her eyes and set her bottle on the floor. "Just don't come crying to me when mat burns cover your legs."

Kiki wrinkled her nose. She hadn't thought of that. She shrugged. She ended up with those, no matter what she wore.

"Okay. I won't." Kiki clapped her hands together. "All right, master of all things diabolical. I want to learn that fancy move."

Lena just shook her head and chuckled.

"Come on, Lena." Kiki hated the whiny sound of her voice. "I've been working with you for months. Can't you at least show me what you did? It didn't look that hard."

Kiki held Lena's gaze as she approached, not willing to show any sign of weakness. Lena circled Kiki, poking her in the shoulder like she was checking for muscles. Lena stopped when she got in front of Kiki and crossed her arms.

"It's not a rookie move, Cookie." Lena lifted her

eyebrow. "You have to advance toward your opponent in order for it to work. Think you could handle that?"

Kiki swallowed the doubt in her throat and nodded.

"All right. Let's train." The smile that spread across Lena's face looked more predatory than friendly.

Kiki's palms slicked with sweat. She could do this and prove that she was tougher than some flaky pastry. She just hoped she survived the next hour without breaking something.

# FIVE

KIKI ROLLED her shoulders as Lena turned to stir whatever magic she cooked on the stove for dinner. Kiki didn't
want to admit it out loud, but she hurt. Everywhere. Lena
had put her through the wringer before she attempted to
teach her the super-duper, bring-down-men-in-one-hit
move. Kiki doubted she could ever pull it off, but she'd
focused on everything Lena said, hoping through some
miracle she could actually do it.

Then, after she'd grabbed a yogurt and apple in the
lounge, she'd gone to the corral to help Derrick. She hadn't
known what to expect, but spending the next hour talking
softly to the horses while Derrick curried and checked their
injuries hadn't been it. He'd said it had taken him the entire
time she'd been with Lena to coax the poor girls into the
stables, and he just needed her to hold their bridles so he
could tend their wounds. Her cheeks heated, remembering
his off-handed comment about her sweet voice soothing the
scared mares.

Unlike the hour with Lena, she hadn't wanted that time
in the stables to end. She'd tried to shake off the weight of

disappointment when Derrick had said he didn't need any more help. She really didn't want to muck out filthy stalls, even if every minute with him and the mares had been more settling than any she'd had in a long while.

So, she'd come back to the house, washed the sweat and grime off of her, and put on her flirty summer dress that flared when she spun and her cowgirl boots. She desperately needed to tap into her Texas roots. It wasn't the toe-curling cowboy with a soft spot for helpless animals that had her blaring her country music, longing to do a little two-stepping. Not at all. She'd just been away from home a little too long and wanted to remember the fun she used to have before her world crashed down around her.

She tapped her foot, bouncing her shoulders, and sang along to the Zac Brown Band's *Chicken Fried* as she chopped the sweet peppers for the salad. She had mastered the art of salad making since moving to the ranch. After several inedible dinners and a near house fire, the others had let her focus on putting together the salad for her contribution to dinner most nights. Other nights, she'd order something in.

*Boot Scootin' Boogie* came over the speaker, and Lena groaned. "I don't mind country as a whole, but this honky-tonk stuff is just too much."

Kiki put the knife down and spun twice to her phone and pressed the next button. *Sold* by John Michael Montgomery came on. Kiki smiled and kicked up her heels as Lena covered her ears.

"For the sake of our friendship and your safety, please change it." Lena glared at Kiki, though the smirk on her lips negated the look.

The front door opened as Kiki danced back to her phone.

"Come on, party pooper. This is great music." She clicked her screen to skip to the next tune in the shuffle.

"Hey! I like that song." Derrick came through the front door covered in dirt and looking exhausted. "Reminds me of the fairground dances after the rodeos in high school."

"Lena's against dancing, having fun, and fantastic music." Kiki smiled as she spun in the open space of the living room as the intro for *Flatliner* by Cole Swindell beeped.

One of Kiki's favorites, the fast pace always made her body move. She closed her eyes and lifted her hands as she danced, pretending she was in the dance hall back home. Colorado was cowboy country just as much as Texas was. Maybe she could find some place here to go dancing.

A warm hand spread across her lower back as another grabbed one of her hands. She jumped, her eyes flying wide open. Derrick twirled her into a two-step as he flashed a smile down on her.

Oh, boy.

There went her heart, jigging right out the door.

"Care to dance?" He pulled her up to him, one hand on her back and the other holding her hand against his chest.

Her head felt light, and her smile could probably be seen from Mars. "Absolutely."

"Hang on." He winked, then pushed her out while grabbing her free hand and twisting their hands over her head so she ended with her arms crossed over her chest and her back up against him.

"Whoop!" She laughed as he spun her out and back in and out.

Her cheeks hurt from smiling as he threw her this way and that, sending her behind his back and pretzeling their arms. Derrick's deep chuckle slid to her toes, and if she wasn't moving so fast, she swore they would curl in her boots.

"You go, girl!" Lena hollered from the kitchen where she clapped them on.

Kiki stared up into Derrick's eyes as he pulled her close and two-stepped a circle. His gaze held a twinkle she hadn't seen before. Then, as if he'd caught his breath or was ready to steal hers, he spun her around so many times she lost count. His hand slid behind her neck, and she dipped almost to the ground. He pulled her up with his hand still cradling her head, spun her once, then dipped her the other way, even lower.

Man alive! Could he dance or what?

She'd spent a lot of nights losing her breath at the Texan music halls, and she'd never once danced like this. It was explosive and slow and sexy all at once. She didn't want to think about how the way they moved together was like they'd danced with each other for years. She didn't want her greed for more to taint this amazing moment given to her by one of her best and only friends.

The song had one more chorus, and she desperately wanted it to last longer. He opened his arms wide and spun her around, stopping with their arms tangled between them. He gazed at her through the hole their arms created, and her breath caught in her chest. Was his brain running wild like hers? Probably not. He sent her through a series of spins, her bobbed hair and skirt flaring wide.

She closed her eyes to bring herself back to reality, willing her traitorous heart to stop pounding from his closeness. Her eyes popped opened as he dipped her low, his face inches from hers. The song ended and both their chests heaved as he leaned over her. Her phone unfortunately chose that moment to play *It's Your Love* by Tim McGraw.

Her cheeks turned hot with the sappy words about love sending a shot right through her.

She licked her parched lips and tried to control her breathing. She could not let her crush on Derrick come out into the light, not if she wanted to find her place among this family of friends. His eyes darted to her lips, then his Adam's apple bobbed in his throat.

He jolted her up and spun her back to the counter before letting her go. "Welp, I stink like I rolled in the compost pile. I'm off to shower."

Her nose wrinkled at the pungent smell that she hadn't noticed when he'd held her in his arms. He threw his head back and laughed, saluting to Lena as he jogged downstairs to the guys' floor like it was just another day at the ranch. Maybe to him it was, but to her, she felt like a high-schooler again and the star quarterback had just said hey to her. Kiki leaned against the counter so her knees didn't give out from under her.

"That Derrick." Lena shook her head as she turned back to the stove. "He's always been the first to swing a pretty lady around the dance floor."

Kiki forced a laugh out as her heart tumbled to her toes like a rock kicked off the mountaintop. There was no reason whatsoever for her to get all depressed over the fact that she was just one of Derrick's many dancing partners. That was more than okay with her.

Liar, her heart whispered to her brain.

Yeah, so? Her brain feebly countered.

She shook her head as she went back to assembling the salad. It was definitely time for her to find some diversions away from the ranch. Especially if she wanted to keep her worn out heart intact.

# SIX

DERRICK RUBBED his belly as he made his way to the theater room, glad for a relaxing night doing nothing. Lena's baked salmon was the best. They weren't entirely sure what she did to it, but it was always five-star delicious. Davis especially loved it, being the fishing fanatic that he was.

"Davis is going to cry like a baby when he realizes he missed your salmon, Lena." Derrick chuckled as he walked toward the movie cabinet to grab the remote.

"Mom sent an entire cooler full of fish." Lena jumped into a recliner, tapping something into her phone. "I plan on making a big feast next time everyone is home."

"Great. Then we'll never have salmon again." Derrick grumbled.

It had been several months since one or more of them hadn't been away on some job. Right now Davis and Tina were searching for a lost teenager over by Estes Park with Scout, Tina's Belgian Malinois, a retired military dog that had needed a home. The missing kid's parents had hired help from the private sector, not trusting the local authorities to do a thorough job. Cooper was out in Hawaii doing some kind of reconnaissance for Zeke. Sosimo and June were in Texas working on something to do with her latest invention. Jake was glued to Chloe as she did her summer tour of music festivals. Rafe was who knows where ... probably bowing down at Piper's feet somewhere.

Derrick scowled as he glanced at the movie options. Though he loved that his friends had found happiness with wonderful women, the dynamic at the ranch had shifted from bachelor mayhem to couple paradise. It left him, Davis, Cooper, Lena, and Kiki out flapping in the wind. Sure, all the roommates had a lot of fun together and everyone on the ranch often hung out, but when Davis and Cooper went for a job, if Derrick wasn't working himself, that left him with a bunch of women. He liked ladies as much as the next man, but never having sisters growing up hadn't prepared him for suddenly getting three in his late twenties.

"Oh, no you don't." Kiki snatched the remote from his hand and squeezed between him and the movies. "No shoot 'em up movies tonight."

Kiki looked up at him with her big blue eyes that rivaled the wide-open Montana skies he remembered as a child. Okay, so Kiki couldn't be counted as a sister. The feelings she stirred up definitely wouldn't fly in a family dynamic. Unless the circumstances were marital. Then, the thoughts swirling through his head definitely would fly—like stratosphere-high flying.

"What?" Derrick couldn't remember what they'd been talking about.

She placed her delicate hand on his chest and the remaining thoughts he'd been gathering together fizzled to nothing.

"Please, no shooting or blowing up or punching faces

movies tonight." Kiki shook her head. "I can't take any more violence today."

Derrick glanced at Lena and spread his hands wide in question. "What's she talking about?"

Lena's smile bordered on cruel satisfaction. "Cookie walked in on me flattening Rafe and knocking him out cold." She shrugged. "I think it jarred her."

Kiki jammed her hands onto her hips. "It wasn't just that Kimjomama move."

"Kajukenbo," Derrick and Lena said at the same time.

"Whatever." Kiki threw her hands up. "Then, I had training, bashing my fists into the bag until they hurt. Next, came keeping those poor mares calm so Derrick could fix them." Her voice broke, and she cleared her throat. "Besides, I've watched hours and hours of your movies, and when we aren't watching movies, you all are beating each other up over a football game or mock combat. Heck, even your card games get intense. I just want one night where I can laugh and maybe, heaven forbid, get goosies."

"Goosies are overrated," Lena scoffed.

Derrick didn't know what the heck goosies were, but he wasn't sure if he wanted to be watching something that could cause them. Kiki placed her hand on his chest, and tiny bumps rushed along his skin from her point of contact. Oh ... goosies.

He took a step back and bowed to cover his unease. "I give all movie choosing rights over to you."

"Really?" Her eyes darted from him to Lena and back. "You two are going to let me pick?"

Did they really run so ramrod over her that she didn't think they'd let her choose a stupid movie? Some friends they were. He rubbed his hand over the back of his neck, trying to erase the discomfort her question brought. Had he become a bully in their friendship, always forcing his way?

He'd had a brilliant afternoon. With Kiki's help, tending to the horses had been easy rather than the fight he'd expected. Shoot, her peaceful whispering to the mares had slid into his gut and settled his frazzled nerves that always zinged for days after a rescue. When he'd come in and swung her into his arms, it had been the perfect cap to a successful day. It wasn't her, not really. Two-stepping with any dancer as talented as Kiki would've made him happy. Most likely.

Derrick plopped on to the couch, determined to be a better friend to Kiki than he had been. She paced in front of the movies, mumbling something to herself. The crinkle in her forehead was adorable, like the movie she picked was a matter of life or death. His eyebrows furrowed. Maybe to the soft-hearted woman it was.

"So, bad day?" Derrick pulled the handle to the footrest and reclined back.

"Huh?" Kiki stopped her pacing.

Man, she really was focused.

"You had a bad day?"

"No, not really." Kiki began pacing again. "Actually, it was pretty good. It's just seeing Rafe laid out like he was and spending an hour learning how to neutralize an unknown enemy kind of rattled me."

Lena snorted, earning a glare from Kiki, which Lena missed with her head buried in her phone. "You are far from neutralizing anything, let alone an enemy."

Kiki's shoulders slumped, and Derrick wished he could knock Lena over the head. Kiki wasn't ex-military like the rest of them. Up to last fall, she'd been nothing but a pampered socialite, someone they'd most likely be hired to protect. He admired she was trying to become stronger and had moved from under her parents' influence.

Kiki shrugged and clicked the TV on. "I may not be able to counter an attack yet, but I will."

He hoped she never had to.

"Speaking of training." Lena lowered her phone and looked at Derrick. "I'm starting a new assignment tomorrow. I have the good fortune of posing as a nanny. It looks like it might last a while. Think you could take over Kiki's training for me?"

"Oh, no." Kiki shook her head, her brown hair flying out around her shoulders. "Derrick has enough on his plate. I don't want to bother him with that."

"I don't mind helping." Derrick held Kiki's gaze, hoping to convey he wanted to. While he was at it, he'd make sure her training was up to par.

She stared at him, making his core heat and his skin itch. She nodded, then took a deep breath like she was preparing for something.

"Okay. You can train me, but only if you let me help you too." She bit her lower lip.

Was she nervous he'd refuse? He honestly wasn't sure how she could help him, but whatever she suggested, he'd go with.

"What are you thinking?"

"Well, two things actually." Kiki twisted her hands in front of her. "One, I know funding your rescues has been a struggle. I'd like to help. Either show you how to make your accounts grow or manage it for you, if you'd like."

"Okay. After you show me what it is you do, I'll let you manage the accounts for me. If you think you can make them grow, that is." He didn't enjoy accounting anyway, so if she could get his money to grow and keep it in order, he was all for it.

She beamed at him like he'd just bought her a flying unicorn. "Great."

He cleared his throat, not wanting her gratitude to settle as warmth in his gut. "Two?"

"Two?" Kiki's eyes widened. "Right. I'd like to help with those two mares, even if it's just to help muck out stalls or what not."

"You want to wade in manure?" Lena chuckled.

Derrick scowled at Lena. She'd grown so cynical and biting since Ethan had died. She may have an edge on her, but that didn't mean she had to be so cutting on everyone else, Kiki especially.

"Yeah, y'all, I want to." Kiki motioned her hand in the barn's direction. "Spending time with those animals today made me happy, like maybe my fear of the colossal beasts was all for nothing. I want to help, even if it means I get covered from head to toe in poo."

"You'll have to get work clothes." Lena motioned her finger up and down Kiki's body. "Your idea of a cowgirl get-up won't work in the stables."

Kiki shrugged. "You'll be gone. I'll just borrow some of your clothes." She wiggled her eyebrows up and down, causing Lena to laugh.

Kiki flopped on to the other side of the couch, stretching her bare feet out so they sat on the cushion next to him. The desire to grab them and place them on his lap burned so hot, he tucked his hands behind his head so he wouldn't give in to the temptation.

She smiled over at him. "Are you ready for one of the best movies ever made?"

"Best movies ever? That's a pretty strong statement."

"What could be better than Lucille Ball, Desi Arnaz, and a road trip from hell?" Kiki held the remote up and pressed the search button. "*The Long, Long Trailer.*"

"Lucille Ball, as in *I Love Lucy*?" Lena groaned. "You mean we have to watch a movie that's a hundred years old?"

"No, not a hundred, and don't complain." Kiki settled into her spot, her feet resting up against Derrick's leg. "I've watched so many of your movies, I'm now dreaming about them. Trust me, it's not the dreams I like having."

The movie started, and Derrick had to admit the antics of the red-headed comedian had him laughing. As he relaxed at the couple's classic comedy and the ridiculousness of pulling a huge trailer cross country behind a car, he decided maybe deviating from the normal movie choices wasn't such a bad thing. It was better than the princess movies Eva often forced him to watch.

After about five minutes into the movie, Derrick gave in to temptation and casually lowered his hand so it rested on Kiki's feet. His heart beat wildly in his chest like some high schooler pulling his first moves on a girl. She didn't seem to even notice. Still, he kept his hand there, wondering if her feet had scarred from when she'd beaten them against the car door trying to get away from her cousin—wondering if they were ticklish, or what she'd do if he started massaging them. All things he shouldn't be thinking about his friend.

# SEVEN

SWEAT GATHERED at the base of Kiki's neck and ran a cold line down her spine, making her shiver. She hadn't even entered the training room, and she was perspiring like a pig. Why in the world had she agreed to this? Her nerves had fired on high alert all morning, causing her to lose focus during her trading. What would Derrick think of her?

She'd spent ten minutes just picking out what to wear ... to workout. The skorts hadn't even gotten looked at. She'd save those for when she ran on the treadmill. She'd finally settled on a pair of black leggings and her black racerback tank. The plain outfit shouldn't get any gruff.

She rolled her eyes at herself for the hundredth time that morning. Since when had Derrick given her any grief about what she wore? She hated that she wanted to impress him. Hated that she felt like the new girl in the high school movies that desperately desired to be part of the in-crowd but ended up with spaghetti on her new blouse after making a fool of herself. Kiki had never been that girl—ever. She'd always connected with the girl wearing a clinging jock draped across her shoulder. The girl who wanted to help the newcomer but was afraid to go against her friends.

When had she allowed fear to permeate her life? Her fear of rejection had determined everything she'd done growing up. Now, it taunted her in this new life she found herself in. She didn't want it squeezing her throat closed and forcing her lips into a fake smile anymore. She wanted confidence in herself that her friends liked her because of who she was. Nothing more than that—not her money, her wardrobe, or the way she looked. So, how did she get to that point?

She stared at the floor as she stepped through the door to the training room, her mind running in a million directions. Two strides in, hands wrapped around her neck from behind. She exploded—her arm swinging and knee striking without her even thinking. She'd made it halfway down the hall to the front door when she heard Derrick's call.

"Kiki, wait." His voice sounded strained.

She stopped and turned, her eyes going wide as he pushed up from the floor. "Oh, no." She rushed back to him and slid under his arm to help him stand. "I'm so sorry."

He rubbed the side of his head where she'd elbow-jabbed him. Great. She hadn't remembered Lena's number one rule: Know your surroundings at all times. She'd failed class before it even started.

"I'm not. You did awesome." Derrick chuckled. He winced and placed his hand on his side. "Perfect, actually. You not only escaped, but made it so I couldn't pursue right away. You gave yourself the head start needed to survive."

"But ... but ... " Her skin tingled, and she tightened her grip on Derrick's waist so she wouldn't collapse in amazement.

She didn't know what to say. His reaction was

completely opposite of what she'd expected. He smiled down at her, and her knees almost buckled. Maybe training under Derrick wouldn't be so bad after all. He squeezed her shoulder and stepped away. She missed the connection, the feel of his warmth pressed against her.

*Don't be a ninny, Kiki.*

"So, we know what you did right." Derrick assumed the soldier-in-control stance all the Stryker team had perfected. "What did you do wrong?"

Kiki crossed her arms, then dropped them to her side, not wanting to show how nervous she was. "I was lost in my thoughts, not aware of my surroundings. I should've known right away that you were hiding, waiting to scare the living daylights out of me. If I had, I wouldn't have hurt you ... much, anyway. I may have still hit you just because."

"Fair enough." Derrick smirked, then stifled it. "Anything else?"

Kiki glanced up at the ceiling, then closed her eyes. What else could she have done? She replayed the terrifying moments in her mind.

"I should've looked back after I got away to assess the situation." She couldn't help the inflection in her tone that made the statement more of a question.

Derrick shook his head. "No, you did right. Once you get loose from an attack, you run like hell and get help." He let his smile free. "I was just testing you. Honestly, Kiki, aside from not being aware of your surroundings, you executed everything perfectly."

Her head filled with so much joy she was sure it'd explode. She'd been working hard trying to learn what Lena drilled into her, but Kiki had honestly thought she was still hopeless. From Lena's expressions, her friend hadn't been impressed with Kiki's attempts either.

"Don't let the familiarity of home let your guard down, though. We're about as secure as you can get here at the ranch, but there's always a possibility someone will breach our defenses." Derrick's reprimand deflated her joy in one whoosh. "You ready to train?"

Kiki nodded, her earlier nervousness flaring back to life.

"Good, we'll begin with some hand-to-hand combat so I can see what Lena's been teaching you, then we'll execute some run-fight-run series."

Derrick motioned her to join him in the center of the mat. Kiki inhaled deeply, pushed her fear aside, and determined to throw herself fully into the experience.

An hour later, she sprinted across the pasture. Sweat saturated her top and slicked her bobbed hair back. She sucked in air like it was being rationed, while Derrick ran next to her like he was out for a Sunday stroll.

Training with Derrick was horrendous.

This was the second time he'd had her do his run-fight-run routine, and she had to say, she wasn't impressed. The attacking of the punching bag for a minute, sprinting a half mile, hitting a bag for another minute he'd thrown on the ground, running another half mile, hug-carrying a fifty-pound bag of grain for a minute, then finally running another half mile had just about killed her the first time. Would she even finish this time?

She had jumped onto the bag on the ground about a quarter mile back. Well, more flopped than jumped, but she hadn't cared at that point. She'd almost not gotten up, just lain down and stayed there for the rest of the day. Yet Derrick's yelling at her like she was some bootcamp recruit had her scrambling to her feet and rushing to the stables for the next torture round.

The bag of grain came into view, and she inwardly

groaned. Derrick glanced her way. Oops. Guess that groan wasn't just in her head. She stumbled up to the table he had the grain waiting on and huffed as the mares nickered at her from the corral. It was easy for them to laugh. They weren't being run through the trenches by Sergeant Battle-Ax.

She missed Lena. Kiki squatted on shaky legs and lifted the heavy bag. Tears formed in her eyes as her arms trembled so violently she wasn't sure she could hang on. She blinked the tears away and gritted her teeth through the pain. One more leg of this course from hell, and she could go cry in the privacy of her shower.

The instant Derrick said go, she dropped the bag in the dirt and raced back toward the training center. Her shoes slapping on the tile floor sounded like freedom. She slowed to a walk as she passed into the training room and dropped to the mat on her back with her arms spread wide. She'd just lay here for a while ... possibly forever since her legs most likely wouldn't work again.

Derrick placed his hands on his head as he strolled into the room. He'd stripped off his shirt in the hot afternoon sun. The only thing that had kept her from ogling him had been the workout only someone truly diabolical would come up with. Now, the fact that he didn't even look out of breath had her closing her eyes in frustration. Someday, maybe, she could run that course and not bat an eye.

"Come on, Sonic." Derrick walked his legs on the outside of hers, bent down, pushed his hands under her back, and picked her up.

She spread her hands on his chest and shamelessly leaned into him when her legs refused to solidify. Her muscles felt like flambéed pudding—painfully on fire and jiggly all at once. What had he said again?

"Sonic?" She let her head flop back on her neck to look at him.

"Yeah, you know that video game?" Derrick peered down at her with a smile. "You didn't tell me you were fast."

"I am?" Why had thinking suddenly become so hard to accomplish?

"Yeah. You ran those half miles in under three and a half minutes each. Few can do that, especially with the punching and lifting thrown in."

Had she really done that? A tiredness that was more fulfilling rather than exhausting spread through her. He raised his eyebrows and went to step away. When her legs buckled, he wrapped his arm around her back to support her. Her impressing him flew right out the window.

"You need to walk it off so your muscles don't seize up." Derrick slowly worked his way toward the door, practically dragging her with him.

"Too late." She grimaced as fire shot up her calves and thighs. She'd be feeling this for days.

"I probably pushed you too far." Derrick's worried tone had her strengthening her spine.

"No. I'm okay. I know better than to collapse like that after a run."

"Why don't we go up to the house? You can take a shower or, better yet, a bath, and relax."

"I'm supposed to help you this afternoon with the horses." Kiki wasn't sure how she'd do it, but she would.

"Kiki, you don't have to help me today."

Disappointment hung heavily on her with his words. She stopped as they stepped back out into the sun and placed her hand on his chest. They both reeked of sweat and dirt. She should be embarrassed that she was so close to him smelling and looking like she did, but she wanted him to see how important it was to her that she help him. So she ignored the heat that spread into her palm and made sure his gaze connected with hers before she spoke.

"Derrick, I want to help those mares." She leaned in closer. "It's important to me. Really important. A couple of ibuprofen, and I'll be fine."

He held her gaze. His hand covered hers still resting on his chest. Why was it so important to her when he'd given her an out? Was it the mares or him? She pushed the thought away, not wanting to dive into her reasons.

He squeezed her hand and nodded. "Okay. I'm going to take a quick shower, grab a snack, then head down to the barn. You can join me whenever you're ready."

Kiki nodded, then turned toward the house so he couldn't see her relief. Her need to help him rooted deeper than the horses, though she had a connection with them she hadn't expected. If she wasn't careful, this entrenched desire for Derrick Nicholson may just be what toppled her.

# EIGHT

DERRICK STIFLED a smile as Kiki grunted in the stall next to him. He'd gotten three stalls mucked out, and she still worked on her first. The way her face had scrunched up when he pointed to the filthy stall had been classic. Why did she have such a burning need to help? It'd just end up dirtying her shiny cowgirl boots.

Her head peeked up from behind the stall wall. She stretched her neck, then extended her arms out in front of her, pulling on each elbow. Why couldn't he tear his gaze from the graceful curve of her neck? She paused as she caught him staring, and Derrick's face heated. Thank God for bad lighting and dark skin.

"Sore?" He chuckled, hoping the tone of his voice didn't sound off.

She stepped to the wall separating them, groaned, and leaned her forehead on the top of her hands that gripped the corral wall. "I think I'll be sore for weeks."

Her muffled words pulled him up short. Had he pushed her too far? He'd only wanted to see what she was capable of.

*Liar.*

He shook his head. She had walked in to the training room, looking hot as all get out, and every cell in his body had overheated. He'd pushed her because he hadn't known how to ignore the spark of attraction that flared to a flame. His workout from hell had more to do with his need to prove they were too different—that she couldn't keep up with him—then he could remember why they were better off as friends.

She'd surprised him, though. First, in her counterattack when he'd grabbed her from behind, and then in her ability to finish the aggressive training many soldiers didn't finish as quickly as she did the first time, let alone twice in a row. Guilt thickened in his throat, making it hard to swallow. In his own discomfort, he'd caused her pain. Some friend he was.

"I know what would make it better." Derrick leaned against the wall with his shoulder as she turned her head and laid her cheek on her hands.

"A bottle of drugs and a head-to-toe massage?" She wiggled her eyebrows up and down.

He swallowed and forced a laugh. The very thought of a massage had his brain veering into places he shouldn't want to go.

"Not quite. What if we head over to Iron Mountain Hot Springs after we work the mares? The minerals in the water will do wonders for your sore muscles."

Though, now that the idea had completely formed in his head, hanging out with her in a bathing suit might not be the best idea, either. Her face lit up, reminding him of Eva when she got the sugar cereal her mother had banned. No matter his discomfort, he couldn't take the suggestion back now.

"I haven't been there yet." Kiki stood, her shoulders rising to her ears as she danced a little gleeful jig. "Piper and Chloe say it's amazing. We've been meaning to get a girls' day out together, but it just hasn't happened."

"Well, we can see who else wants to come." Pathetic how he hoped she said no to that suggestion.

"Zeke and Sam are having a family night tonight. They promised Eva they'd take her to the fairy caverns. Piper's morning sickness keeps her close to the bathroom, so she and Rafe are out. Everyone else is gone." Kiki tipped her head. "Why do they call it morning sickness if she's sick all the time?"

"No clue." Derrick pushed off the wall, relieved more than he should be that everyone was either gone or busy. "Well, it's just the two of us then. No action-packed movie tonight."

"Thank goodness." She smiled, then scanned her stall with a furrowed forehead.

Derrick jumped in before she could continue cleaning it. "It's clean. Let's go see how my new girls are doing."

"You sure?" She peered over the wall at the stall he'd cleaned. "It doesn't look as good as yours."

"It's fine. You know me. I go a bit overboard on things."

She pushed her mouth to the side like she was trying not to laugh. The urge to bend over the wall and kiss the dimple that she couldn't quite hide had him rushing out of the stall to hang the tools up. She was his friend, nothing more, especially since he wasn't sure if he was staying with Stryker or leaving. It'd be selfish to start something, then later, if he left, make her choose between him or her family here at the ranch.

He wasn't about to let this momentary lapse in judgement make things harder on her. Disappointments and discomforts had riddled her life for the last year. He didn't want to add himself to that.

# NINE

KIKI MARVELED at the small pools dotting the landscape before her that seemed to blend perfectly with the red and tan mountains and sagebrush that led to the Colorado River past the spa's fence. Country music played quietly over speakers, which Kiki wholeheartedly approved of. Everything about the facility screamed relaxation. Even the larger swimming pool fit the whole rejuvenation vibe with its curved shape and waterfall wall at the far end.

Excitement had bubbled out of her as she had gathered her things at home to come. She hadn't wanted to waste a moment, so she'd dressed in her bathing suit under her sundress to quicken her entrance into luxury. Now, though, she was ready, and Derrick wasn't anywhere to be seen. Should she hop into a soaking pool and hope he found her?

She bit her lip as a group of guys approached. She should just find the nearest pool and get in. She could always wave like mad when Derrick finally came out from the bathhouse.

One man from the group walking toward her stopped

and smiled. He had defined muscles, a killer smile, and what she'd imagine romance writers would consider smoldering eyes. He wore a cowboy hat that was the complete opposite of his swimsuit, but somehow he pulled it off. He was exactly the kind of guy she'd be flirting with back home, trying to get a first date from. Yet, since meeting Derrick, her usual specimens of attraction paled in comparison. Didn't that just suck since Derrick was a no-go for her if she wanted to stay at the ranch?

"Hey, darlin'. You lost?" Handsome-in-a-hat's forehead scrunched up like he was concerned.

"Nope, thanks. Just waiting for a friend."

"Well, anyone who'd keep an angel like you waiting isn't much of a friend." He stepped closer, and Kiki rolled her eyes. "I was just leaving, but I could hang out. Show you a good time."

The man winked. Kiki snorted. Was this guy serious? Derrick's familiar scent surrounded her and a warm hand spread across her back, sending shivers of delight up her spine.

"Sorry I kept you waiting." Derrick's voice held a slight tightness she'd never heard before.

His jaw clenched as he smiled down at her. Kiki's eyebrows pushed together. Was she missing something? His words were just a friendly apology, but his arm around her waist and his tight smile to the eager cowboy made it seem like there was something more between her and Derrick.

Her eyes widened, and her fingers tingled. Was this a date, like a date-date? She hadn't gotten that vibe on the way over, but then again, her judgement around him seemed to fly out the window.

He turned his gaze to her, his eyes softening. "Ready?"

He flexed his fingers on her back, shooting sparks along

her skin. What in the world was happening? She stood there frozen. All rational thought vacated, leaving only confusion and joy battling in her head.

"Yeah. Sure," she squeaked out from her parched throat.

"Come on. Let's go relax." He nodded to the group of men and stepped past the cowboy who Kiki had forgotten still stood there with a glare on his face.

"Okay," she whispered.

Once they got past the rest of the guy's friends, Derrick let go of her waist and threaded his fingers through hers. Kiki's pulse beat painfully against her throat, and she worried she'd pass out on the way to the water. Wouldn't that be ironic, fainting at a rejuvenation spa? Though, she probably didn't need the healing waters now. His touch dulled all the pain in her body, like some kind of magic pill.

Derrick glanced over his shoulder at the bathhouse and dropped her hand like it had burned him. "Sorry about that." He cleared his throat. "I've seen guys like that before, lurking and pouncing on every unattached woman."

Reality washed over her like she'd jumped in the cold Colorado River. He'd just been protecting her after all. Their status quo hadn't changed, and she was foolish to think it had.

She glanced away, blinking quickly to hide the silly tears that had sprung up with his words. *Don't make this awkward, Cookie. Don't be a cream puff.*

She gave him a weak smile. "Thanks, though I probably could've handled it. I'm kind of used to guys hitting on me."

Why'd she have to say that? She didn't want to act like some entitled, pouting diva. She cocked her eyebrow and crossed her arms. Maybe if she acted perturbed, he wouldn't see her hands trembling.

His dark brown eyes gazed down at her with an intensity she didn't understand. He blinked and nodded, a mask of calm replacing the emotion. Oh, for the ability to read minds.

"Yeah, I bet you are." He jerked his eyes away and pointed at an empty pool. "How does that one look?"

"Perfect." She stalked over, dropped her towel and water bottle in the rocks surrounding the pool, and stepped into water, all without looking at Derrick.

She couldn't. Not until she got her emotions under control. This was supposed to be a fun and relaxing outing with a friend. Not a torturous trip to Want-But-Can't-Haveville.

She sank into the hot water with a sigh. She just needed to chill out and let the minerals leech all her frustrations from her. Derrick scanned the area, then stepped into the pool. Her eyes skirted across his dark skin, admiring his muscles that rippled with each move.

*Oh, dear Lord in heaven, help me.*

This outing proved more treacherous to her heart than she imagined possible. Her face heated, and not from the steaming water. As she willed her brain to turn her eyes away from ogling his bare chest, her gaze stumbled over the scars that riddled his body. A cluster of puckered skin right above his hip bone. A line slashing across his chest. What looked like a burn on his thigh and lower back.

She jerked her gaze to her hands distorted under the water so she couldn't see the reminders of his violent past —couldn't imagine the possibility of future injuries with the job he had. Why had her friends continued to put themselves in danger after they got out of the military? Weren't they tired of the risk, of the chance of not coming home from a job? What was it that made them different from her? She could hardly watch a movie about war without feeling ill and having nightmares, and yet Derrick and his friends continued to run into danger like there was nothing to it. They wore honor like a second skin. With the taint of her family and her scaredy-cat nature, she doubted she'd ever have even a semblance of what they had.

He positioned himself next to her on the river side of the pool, facing the walkway. He'd picked the pool closest to the property line and the smallest one there. It wasn't a romantic move, though she wished it was, but a strategic one. He'd situated them where it'd be hard to sneak up from behind, and only about two more people could fit without crowding. Would he even be able to relax, or would he be on alert the entire time they were here?

She closed her eyes and laid her head against the rounded edge of the pool. She'd leave with muscles more sore than when she got here if she didn't put the worry behind her. If Derrick wanted to stand guard, that was his choice. At least with him around, she wouldn't be called to use her new defensive skills, not that she'd had to use them before or since her cousin's attack.

The fright of that day and the pain that had radiated from her feet for weeks assaulted her brain. Why'd she have to go thinking about that? She dunked her head under the roasting water, washing away the troubling memories with a shake of her head. When she came up and wiped the moisture from her face, she found Derrick staring at her.

"You okay?" Of course, Derrick, aka Mother Goose, would notice her discomfort.

Nothing ever got past him. That thought stalled her brain to a halt. Had he noticed her little crush? If he had, he hadn't let on.

"Yeah. Just thinking."

"Must not have been a very good thought, from your expression."

She shrugged, not really wanting to talk about it. She hadn't ever talked about it, at least not past telling the district attorney what had happened. Her father's lawyers would keep the case locked in a perpetual hold as long as feasible. Heck, she might never testify, but maybe she shouldn't keep it all bottled up anymore. That whole challenge to face her fears and become a stronger person really sucked sometimes.

She settled her head back on the edge, closed her eyes, and allowed her body to float to the surface of the water. "I was just thinking how you're always on guard, how I won't ever get to use those new skills you and Lena are teaching me with you around." She shrugged. "The only time I've ever needed to defend myself was against Gregory. We all know how that ended up. I guess the memory of that day and the weeks after kind of overwhelmed me for a moment."

"You were strong, Kiki." Derrick's soft voice settled in her bones, relaxing her even more. "You fought like a wildcat and didn't give up even with your feet covered in blood and swollen."

"Yeah, well, now I'll be stronger."

He moved from her side, and Kiki dared to open her eyes. His hand skimmed along her calf, shooting fire up her leg. Holy moly, this man lit her on fire and didn't even know it. He gently cupped her heels in his giant hands, and she forced herself not to move, to just float there as he examined her feet.

"You could do some damage to anyone attacking you now, that's for sure." His mouth twitched up at the side and her head about slipped from the pool's edge. "When I'm done with you, you'll be deadly."

That image both terrified and exhilarated her. Could little ol' her really have the power to hurt someone that badly? She rolled her eyes and snorted. Not likely.

A wicked smile pushed his lips up. "Don't doubt my training ability."

He grabbed both her ankles with one hand and tickled her feet with the other. She shrieked, her head dunking under water as she tried to get away. She came up sputtering and laughing, desperate to get out of his hold.

"Sir. Miss." A wide-eyed pool attendant rushed up to the water's edge. "Rough housing needs to be taken to the family pool, please."

"Sorry." Derrick snickered as he dropped her ankles, giving her a little push under.

Her head submerged beneath the surface with the sudden release of her legs. Why that—he'd pay. She tried not to laugh underwater. Derrick pulled her up, his arm anchored around her back. Merriment rushed from her in one tangible whoosh. Oh, the fates were evil, giving her a friend who stole her heart. He reached up with his free arm and clumsily pushed her hair out of her face. She couldn't breathe, not with him pressed so close to her.

"I don't want you to worry about being able to defend yourself anymore." His voice sounded husky and deeper than normal. "You're good, getting better every day."

She nodded, not knowing what he meant or how she should respond. She licked her lips, suddenly parched like she trekked through the desert instead of being surrounded by water. His eyes darted to her mouth.

He cleared his throat and stepped away, sitting on the

pool's underwater bench and closing his eyes. "No more horsing around, Kiki. We're here to relax."

Kiki laughed, swatted him on the arm, and settled in next to him. Maybe he wasn't as unaffected by her as she thought. The possibility buoyed her more that the healing waters ever could.

# TEN

THE FOLLOWING MORNING, Derrick finished adhering his fake scar to his back. Now that he had retired from the Army, he would probably never need the razor blade and handcuff keys he glued to his body every day and concealed beneath the silicone scars on his back and calf. Two years after getting out, he still took the time each morning for the ritual.

He glanced at the clock. 0530 "Shoot."

He was late.

He rushed out of his room and dashed up the stairs. He'd have to eat something later. He didn't want to keep Kiki waiting any longer. He bypassed the kitchen, taking the stairs to the second story two at a time.

His eyes widened as he stepped into Kiki's office. He hadn't been upstairs since the women took it over, and the change to his old bedroom surprised him. His style was pretty basic. Bed with a dark comforter, nightstands, and a dresser was enough for him. The pictures of his family on his dresser were the only decorations.

His old bedroom under Kiki's hand had transformed

completely. Four plasma screens hung from the wall painted a pale yellow over a desk with a bright turquoise pencil holder, matching file folders neatly displayed in a rack, and a diffuser shooting steam into the air. On a table on the opposite side of the room, coffee brewed in a French press, an electric tea kettle steamed, and a vase of freshly cut wildflowers brightened the already cheery space. The scent of peppermint and coffee energized him more than the jog upstairs had.

What surprised him most and threw him sideways was Kiki on her knees with her back bent in an impossible angle where her head sat on the ground between her feet. Her body was bent into a bridge on steroids. Man, she was incredible. She kept amazing him, kept him second-guessing his decision to just stay friends.

She smiled up at him. "I just have two more poses then I'll be done. I'm a little behind this morning."

He leaned against the doorjamb. "I didn't know you were part pretzel. What is that pose anyway?"

"King Pigeon, and don't talk about food. I'm hungry." She chuckled as she effortlessly lifted from the pose and moved into an even harder position.

With her elbows supported beneath her belly and her hands on the floor under her hips, she balanced like a flat teeter-totter. After the day before, he knew she had strength, but he'd never seen anyone do moves like these so effortlessly. Was her air conditioning not working? Because he was burning up. He tore his gaze away from her as she folded into the only yoga move he knew, the child's pose.

"There's fresh coffee." Kiki's muffled voice pulled his eyes right back to her. "I brought up a mug for you."

Was she always this thoughtful, or was she still vying for acceptance here? It hadn't escaped his notice how she bent over backwards trying to fit in. She was subtle about it. The others might not even see it, but he had. Would she ever believe that they wanted her here because she was family, no matter what had happened in the past?

"Thanks." He stepped in and turned his back to her.

He needed to get a grip. Today wasn't any different from every other day since she'd arrived. His sudden inability to not stop thinking about her wouldn't affect their friendship. He'd make sure of that.

"Want me to pour your mug?" He peeked over his shoulder as she rolled up her yoga mat.

"Yeah, thanks. There's also yogurt and fruit in the fridge in the closet. Want me to grab you some?"

"Sure."

She disappeared into the closet with her mat, and he took a deep breath for the first time since stepping up to the door. What if there was something between them? She hadn't ever flirted with him beyond the playful joking of friends. The memory of her pulled close to him in the pool paused his hand as he stirred in Kiki's creamer. The way her gaze had held his for that space of time when he'd wanted to bend down and kiss her said she might not be against a change in their relationship.

He shifted on his feet as he set down the spoon and picked up the mugs. He'd have to be cautious though, examine all the angles before he decided to pursue something more with her. He couldn't risk making her uncomfortable here at the ranch. Being with Eva was important to Kiki, and he wouldn't mess that up for anything.

She emerged from the closet with two yogurts, two apples, and a devious smirk on her beautiful face. "You ready for a crash course in day trading?"

"No. It's too early for math." He'd always hated school,

and the thought of being stuck sitting at a desk all morning should've had him itching for open air.

Kiki tipped her head back, and her joyful laugh filled the space, soothing down his nerves. The outdoors were overrated. Staying inside with her would be worth missing the sunshine.

She nodded her chin toward the chairs at the desk. "Welcome to my battlefield."

They sat at the desk and for the next three hours she blurred his brain with trading mumbo jumbo. She showed him how she determined which trades to make, how a conservative approach—rather than the frantic image of traders on Wall Street—profited, and what she proposed to do with his funds. Her returns on her own trading were staggering, and he'd be a fool if he didn't let her grow his funds for his rescue project.

"So, what do you think?" Kiki pushed back from the desk with her hands wrapped around her cold mug of coffee. She maintained eye contact, but the deep breath she took before continuing revealed her vulnerability. "It's fine if you need time to think or you decide not to let me see what I can do. There's definitely a risk involved, so I can understand if you don't—"

"Kiki, you're brilliant." His words relaxed her tight expression. "It's obvious you know what you're doing. I'd be royally stupid not to let you have a go at it."

"So, you want me to manage your funds?"

"Yeah, and if you're up to it, I'll give you my personal savings too." He motioned to the screens and her paperwork. "What you've got going on is a heck of a lot better than my current portfolio."

She sighed and relaxed into her chair. "Thanks, Derrick. I'll do everything—"

Her phone rang, interrupting her. She looked at the screen, her forehead furrowing before she answered.

"Hey, Sam. What's up?"

Derrick and Kiki sat close enough he could hear Sam through the phone. "Kiki, could you watch Eva today? Zeke and I are going to Aspen to meet with a potential client, and with Piper still so sick, I don't want her and Rafe to have to mess with Eva."

"Absolutely. Y'all know I love any time I get to spoil—I mean play with Eva." Kiki's face radiated excitement. "Maybe I'll take her to that park in town and go for ice cream after."

"Well ... I ... I don't know." Sam waffled, and Kiki's countenance fell.

"I'll go with you." Derrick tapped Kiki's foot.

Her closed-mouth smile held no true happiness to it. "Sam, Derrick says he'll come with us."

Kiki picked at her leggings as she waited for Sam to answer. Her earlier confident posture vanished completely.

"That will work perfect. Tell Derrick thanks, and thank you for keeping her at such short notice," Sam gushed through the phone.

"I don't mind helping at all." Kiki shifted the phone to her other ear. "You and Eva are everything to me."

Sam said something else that Derrick couldn't hear, and Kiki ended the call. She turned the phone in her hand before placing it on her desk. Her fingers trembled as she pulled her hand away, and Derrick wanted to lace his fingers with hers.

"Do you think they'll ever trust me enough to have Eva without a babysitter?" Kiki's forlorn tone broke his heart.

"It's not you, Kiki."

She snorted.

"Really. Even Sam doesn't take Eva away from the ranch without Zeke." Derrick wanted her to see the truth. "They're still worried your parents will try something else."

"Not with the media hounding them, they won't."

Derrick couldn't not comfort her anymore. He placed his hand on her shoulder and slid it across her back. He wanted her to see the truth, that their caution had nothing to do with her.

"Trust me." He held her stare, praying the doubt shining there would erase with his words. "No one leaves the ranch with Eva alone. We're all paranoid, but it's not a distrust in you. You're family now, one of us."

Tears filled her eyes before she blinked them away. "Thanks, Derrick." She stood and set her mug on the desk. "I need to get changed if Eva's coming over soon."

She offered him a weak smile and left the room. The soft click of her bedroom door closing knocked against his chest and stuttered his breath. Somehow he'd prove to her she mattered to them, that she belonged on the ranch and nothing could change that.

# ELEVEN

KIKI, Derrick, and Eva sat on a blanket in the park. Kiki had been surprised that the place was deserted except for a couple of guys that showed up after they did and were hanging out at one of the picnic tables. Maybe it was still too early for families to be out.

They'd just finished packing up the mess from an impromptu picnic breakfast, and Eva bounced on her knees like they had wound her up and she was ready to go. Kiki never knew she could love someone as much as she loved her niece. Her gaze darted to Derrick's face, then back to Eva. She'd learned a lot about love since she'd moved to Colorado.

"Come on, Aunt Kiki," Eva whispered in Kiki's ear loudly. "Let's get Uncle D."

Derrick reclined back on his elbows with his legs stretched out in front of him, surveying the area. He turned his head so he couldn't see Eva, a small smirk on his lips. The surprise attack foiled by a little girl whose excitement raised her voice too loud.

Eva's pleading smile stretched across her dark face, and

her blue eyes that matched Kiki's begged in a way no person with a heart could resist. Kiki lifted her finger to her lips, motioning Eva to be quiet. Eva pressed her fingers to her mouth like she needed to hold the excitement in. Her black curls bounced around her shoulders.

Kiki pulled Eva close. The smell of sunshine and donuts lingering in Eva's hair warmed Kiki to the core. If she could bottle that happy scent, she'd make a fortune.

Kiki whispered quietly in Eva's ear. "I'll take his legs. You get the rest of him."

Eva's expression turned serious as she nodded and rubbed her hands together. Kiki almost lost it, but held the laughter in. She put up her fingers and mouthed, "Three, two, one."

Eva burst from her spot on the blanket with an impressive sound of attack and landed with a thud on Derrick's chest. His groan and stifled chuckle sounded real. Had the five-year-old bested the big, powerful warrior?

Kiki scrambled across the blanket, not wanting to let Eva down. She sat on Derrick's legs, pinning them to the blanket. She had no illusion that Derrick couldn't easily escape. She'd seen him bench press three times what she and Eva weighed combined. Yet, he pretended to struggle for a few seconds before relaxing with an exaggerated sigh.

"You got me." Derrick sounded dejected. "When did you become such a master attacker, Eva-mine?"

"Mommy's been teaching me." Eva bounced on Derrick's stomach in excitement. "We attack Daddy all the time."

"Well, your mom has a lot she can teach you." Derrick chuckled. "Your dad doesn't stand a chance."

Eva beamed and leaned her elbows on Derrick's chest. Though her skin wasn't as dark as Derrick's, the two looked so much alike they really could be family. Unlike Kiki, Eva's real aunt, who appeared nothing like her niece. The only characteristic they shared were their blue eyes. Lots of people had blue eyes.

Kiki shouldn't be jealous of something that couldn't be helped, but shamefully, she was. It would probably be better for Eva if Kiki left. The little girl had family falling from the rafters with all the "uncles" living at the ranch. Kiki's family had caused so much trouble for Sam and Eva already. Maybe if Kiki left, Sam would finally relax her guard a little and not feel like Eva needed security 24/7.

Kiki's late breakfast settled like a ton of bricks in her stomach. Why hadn't she thought that possibility through before? Was she really so selfish that she'd hold on to the happiness she'd found at the ranch, though it might cause Sam and Eva undue stress? With Sam pregnant, she didn't need any added worries. Kiki had some serious praying and analyzing to do when they got home.

"You're pinned, buster." Eva propped her chin on her little fists.

"That I am." Derrick leaned his head to peek around Eva and winked at Kiki. "That was a good surprise attack, munchkin. Kneeing me in a full gut was an especially effective maneuver."

Kiki shook her head. So that had caused the grunt.

"Now that you got me, what are you going to do to me?" Derrick's question had Kiki's face flaming red hot.

She could think of several things she'd like to do to him. None of them were bound to happen anytime soon, so she'd better get her head out of the gutter and focus on whatever diabolical plan her niece cooked up. She couldn't afford for her expression to give her away, especially now that she was contemplating leaving. The thought made her chest ache. Would she be able to pull herself away?

"We'll let you go if you take us to get ice cream." Eva shifted so her hands were on his shoulders, pinning Derrick to the ground.

"Extortion!" His shocked tone was so fake Kiki had to cover her mouth to keep her giggle in.

"No, Uncle D. We won fair and square, now you have to pay up." Eva sat up and placed her hands on her hips.

Derrick lifted his legs straight up, throwing both Eva and Kiki into his chest. Kiki stopped herself from crushing her niece by bracing her hands on either side of Derrick's body. His arms locked around Kiki's back, trapping both her and Eva in his embrace. Man, Kiki wanted this, wanted to be held and loved. Not that Derrick loved her. Eva's gleeful laughter bounced against Kiki's chest, making her giggle as well. The sense of family surrounded her, filling her to the brim with connection.

"Ha, now what are you going to do?" Derrick rocked his arms back and forth, shaking them and making them laugh even louder.

"Wait, stop. I've got to tell you something." Eva shrieked between words she could hardly let out past her merriment.

Derrick stopped, and Eva wiggled like she wanted to climb out of the trap. Derrick loosened his arms. How pathetic that Kiki relished he didn't let go completely. Eva crawled up and pushed Derrick's head to the side so she could whisper in his ear. His eyes twinkled as he looked up at Kiki.

Kiki loved the teasing way all the men of Stryker Security played with Eva. Kiki hadn't had many chances to just be silly growing up with all the expectations her parents had put on her. They'd wanted her brother and her to act like grownups for as long as she could remember. She'd missed out and had determined if she ever had kids, she'd run and be wild with them as long as they'd let her.

Derrick let go of Kiki's waist with one hand and pushed Eva's curls out of his face. Kiki missed his touch. Yet the way he gently placed his hand on Eva's shoulder made Kiki all gooey inside, like a cookie fresh from the oven. Shoot, Lena was right. Kiki was soft as a pastry.

"Uncle D," Eva whispered in a voice that wasn't quiet at all. "Aunt Kiki will buy us ice cream, 'specially if we tickle her. She'll do anything not to be tickled."

Kiki gasped. The little turncoat. She scrambled out of Derrick's grasp, now glad both arms weren't pinning her down.

"First you have to catch me, you little traitor." Kiki took off across the park.

"Get her!" Eva hollered behind Kiki.

She peeked over her shoulder and almost stumbled at Derrick's beaming expression. He scooped Eva up and carried her, chasing after Kiki. Her legs felt light as she swerved in a new direction, her happiness leaving her breathless. Derrick's loud laugh tumbled down inside her and settled in her stomach.

She couldn't leave all this behind, could she? She slowed her pace as she let the two people who meant the world to her close the gap. She wanted them to catch her, to hold her close. She'd give everything she had to keep this joy she'd found in the Colorado mountains, even if that made her the most selfish person alive.

# TWELVE

EVA SWUNG between Derrick and Kiki, her feet kicking high in front of her as they walked back to his vehicle. Her laughter filled him with a joy he hadn't felt since middle school. Kiki giggled, drawing his gaze to her. His chest warmed for an entirely different reason. She smiled up at him, and something shifted in him. Her expression wasn't the hesitant, cautious one she often wore. It shone bright and hopeful.

He wanted to keep the look on her face for the rest of her life.

Eva put her feet on the ground and pulled Derrick and Kiki close, wrapping her little arms around them both in an Eva sandwich. "I love you guys so much."

"Come here, Eva-mine." He scooped her up and set her on his hip. "If we're going to have a group hug, we need to do it properly."

He slid his hand along Kiki's lower back and pulled her close. What was he thinking? She stiffened, then with a sigh, slid one arm around his back and the other around

Eva. She laid her head on his chest with another exhale. He didn't know what he was thinking, but he was sure feeling all kinds of warm tingles he'd never felt before.

"I love you too, Eva." Kiki's whispered words caught as her arm squeezed Derrick. "Love being here with you two."

She tipped her head up, peering at him through long lashes, and Derrick's world stopped right there on the city sidewalk. He tightened his arms and wanted to keep her there with him for the rest of time.

*Whoa! Hold your horses, man.*

His heart beat in his throat, warning him he hadn't thought this through completely yet. Hadn't planned and prepared and studied all possible angles. There was no exit plan that wouldn't leave people hurt in this scenario.

"Is it time for ice cream now?" Eva patted her hand on Derrick's cheek, pulling him off the path he still wasn't sure he should take.

He turned his face to smile at Eva. "Yep. Let's go fill you up with more sugar."

"Yippee!" Eva squeezed them both before squirming to get down.

He set her on the sidewalk, and she skipped in front of them. The back of his hand brushed Kiki's as they followed Eva. What would Kiki do if he captured her hand in his? The desire to do so, to feel her warm skin against his, pushed all other thought aside.

Pain spiked through his head as something hit him from behind. Derrick pushed Kiki toward Eva and turned to confront the attacker. A fist connected with his nose, exploding stars before his eyes. Where had this guy come from? Eva's scream almost covered the skidding of tires on gravel and dropped ice in his gut. He had to neutralize this attacker and get Kiki and Eva safe. He'd been an idiot to let a pretty face distract him.

He used all the power he had to swing his fist into the face of the man he now recognized as one of two that had been hanging out at the picnic table. The dude's head snapped back, and he dropped to the ground. Derrick didn't wait to see if the guy was out but turned to help Kiki.

"No!" Kiki yelled as she turned from her attacker and reached for Eva.

A man jumped from the side door of a van and grabbed Eva around the waist. Derrick's legs threatened to buckle beneath him as Kiki's attacker grabbed her from behind.

"Stop screwing around and get the woman in the van." The man holding Eva barked in Spanish at the other.

"We need them all," the other guy grunted back, wrapping his arm around Kiki's waist.

She exploded, arms and legs connecting with the man that held her. Derrick closed the distance, punching the man in the face and tossing him from Kiki. The cocking of a gun spun him around and stopped his heart.

Eva's big blue eyes were bright with tears. A gun pressed hard against her temple. Derrick would kill the man and everyone else threatening his family.

"Get in the van or I shoot her brains out right here on the sidewalk." Evil shone from the man's dark eyes. He would do it, probably relish the act.

"No, please, I'm coming. Just ... just, let them go." Kiki held her hands up in front of her and stepped up to the van.

Her words slammed into Derrick's gut. He wasn't about to let her get in that van. He'd never see her again. That thought pushed bile up his throat. He should've been on guard. Shouldn't have let her distract him.

"No, you all come." The finality of the man's words eased Derrick's dread.

If they were together, he could keep them safe. Get them out of whatever crazy mess this was. Apart, they were doomed.

"Okay, man. We're coming." Derrick stepped up behind Kiki and placed a hand on her back.

Kiki reached out shaking hands for Eva. The man thrust the child into Kiki's arms, and Eva's shoes fell off her feet in the exchange. Kiki's shoulders shook in a stifled sob as she stepped forward and climbed into the van. Derrick bent down to pick up the only hope of getting help, knowing Zeke had hidden tracking devices in all of Eva's shoes.

"Leave them." The man kicked the shoes into the gutter, the sparkly pink landing in oily mud.

Derrick ducked his head and climbed into the van as his neck muscles tightened with annoyance. Didn't matter. There were other ways of getting free.

They had stripped the inside of the van of all the seats. Kiki cowered in the very back of the space. Good, maybe he could get them out the back doors. He climbed in, positioning himself in front of Kiki where she clung tight to Eva.

"It'll be okay," he whispered as the man who'd attacked Kiki helped his friend from the picnic table into the van.

Her breath shuddered behind him, and Eva's sobbing filled his ears. Did Kiki believe him? He didn't quite believe himself either.

The door slammed closed, and the van sped off with a squeal. Could he take the men out and escape now? There were only four of them, including the driver, and the guy who jumped him wouldn't put up much of a fight. As if sensing his thoughts, the devil who'd held Eva pointed the gun at Derrick's chest and cocked it.

"Why are we messing with this trouble, Edgar?" Devil man spoke in Spanish to his friend but didn't take his eyes off Derrick.

"They're her family." Edgar wiped the blood from his mouth with a grimace. "It's probably why she's been hiding out at that ranch."

"We don't have any intel confirming that." The leader glared at Edgar.

"Matias, I promise. They are. The girl has her blue eyes. We have more leverage with all of them." Edgar smiled at Matias, his teeth covered in blood.

"No ... no." Kiki tried to push past Derrick, surprising them all that she understood the men's Spanish, but he wrapped his arm around her to anchor her behind him. "You're wrong. They aren't my family. We're just friends. They won't give you anything but a headache."

"D—D—" Eva stuttered as she grabbed Derrick's arms.

Derrick's stomach fell at the way Eva sounded like she tried calling him Daddy. Matias's eyes slitted, bouncing from Kiki to Eva to Derrick and back again.

"You will learn not to lie to me." The tightness in Matias's accented English and the set of his jaw had Derrick clenching his fists in response.

"But, I'm not—"

"Shh, honey, it's all right." Derrick cut Kiki off when she sobbed out a protest.

"As for you." Matias leaned toward Derrick. "Hurt my men again, and I will kill you."

Derrick stifled a smirk and slumped his shoulders, holding up his hand in surrender. "S ... sorry, man. Just kind of reacted."

If he could get them to believe that he wasn't a threat, maybe they'd let down their guard. Derrick pretended to tremble. Matias's lip curled in disgust. Derrick would do whatever he had to, even look like a weak fool, if it meant getting Kiki and Eva out of here. Matias's arm swung toward Derrick a second before the gun slammed into his head, and he fell into darkness.

# THIRTEEN

EVA SHRIEKED as Derrick crashed to the floor, and Kiki swallowed her breakfast that threatened to spew. She should've left long ago. Heck, she should've never stayed in the first place. She'd learned just how evil her family was. She shouldn't have kept her friends in danger. Eva sobbed in Kiki's arms, frantically pushing on Derrick.

"Shh, honey. He's okay." Kiki tried to calm Eva though she herself spun, grasping tight to the threads of her emotions as they threatened to rip her already stretched seams apart.

She had to be strong for Eva. Kiki couldn't fall apart, not until she got Eva and Derrick out of this.

She clutched Eva close to her side with one arm and leaned over Derrick, rubbing her hand over his dark, shaved head. He'd lost his cowboy hat during the fight. Not that it mattered now. She winced at the goose egg where the jerk Matias had hit Derrick. Would her family ever stop hurting others?

She knew this had something to do with her father.

Why else would someone need her and her supposed family as leverage? Her hands chilled to ice. If these mercenaries realized that Eva and Derrick weren't Kiki's family, they'd kill them both. They had to pretend and make it convincing. But how would she get a five-year-old to play house when real-life guns were being pressed to her head?

Kiki's hands shook as she bent closer to Derrick and kissed right above his ear. She didn't have to fake the tremble of her lips or the shake of her hands.

"Babe, wake up." She jostled his shoulder, her voice cracking as tears threatened to fall. "Please, wake up."

Derrick groaned and rolled onto his back. His dark brown eyes blinked open, and his forehead scrunched in confusion. Eva started crying harder and threw herself into his chest. Kiki wanted to do the same. Isn't that what a wife or lover or whatever it was these guys thought she was would do?

She buried her face into his neck, her shoulders shuddering in a sob before she clamped down her emotions. "I'm sorry."

His hand threaded through her hair and cupped the back of her head. "It's not your fault. We'll get us home." His whisper barely reached her ear as he leaned his face into her hair. "Let's see if we can get out of this van through the back door."

He hugged her closer before loosening his arm. Kiki didn't want to leave the protection of his arms, her weakness making her sick. She helped him up while their captors spoke rapid Spanish to each other. Good thing her nanny taught her the language right alongside English when she was little. The men were moaning about their injuries. Matias laughed at Edgar, making fun of the fact that Kiki had bested him. Matias still held the gun, loosely pointing it toward the back of the van.

When the airport appeared through the windshield and Matias told the driver to pull up to the airplane, Kiki's palms slicked with sweat. If they didn't escape now, who knew where they'd end up. Samantha and Zeke would kill her.

Derrick sat up and pulled her into a hug. "Can you see the back door?" he whispered softly, and she answered with a small nod. "See if it'll open. If it does, we bail out the back."

He adjusted his position so she was directly in front of the handle. Her heart thrashed in her throat as she reached out her hand and pulled on the handle. The door didn't move, and she whimpered.

"Hey, it's okay." Derrick squeezed her slightly. "Is there a lock?"

She frantically searched around the handle, then the door. Why wasn't there a lock? The van slowed, and dread pooled in her stomach. She had to do something. The side door slid open, causing her to jump.

Matias motioned with the gun. "Out. Don't make me shoot you."

She swallowed, but her mouth and throat were still so dry. She scooted out, letting Derrick keep Eva in his arms. Her heart thundered in her chest as she stared up the stairs leading to the airplane. She couldn't let Eva and Derrick get on that jet. This plane was big enough, they could end up almost anywhere.

She felt Derrick's heat as he stepped up behind her. Poor Eva hiccupped as her sobs slowed. Kiki shifted so she stood between the people she loved and the man threatening them.

"Get in the plane." Matias's cold, deadly eyes pierced her soul.

"These two won't give you any leverage with my father. He hates their existence. Why do you think we've kept our relationship secret?" Kiki stepped forward, pulling away from Derrick's hand as he gripped her arm. "You could leave them locked in the van, and it'll be hours before anyone finds them. We'll be so far gone, no one will know where we've ended up."

Matias sneered as he stepped toe to toe with her, his rank breath hot against her face. "If you speak the truth, we will just kill them." He looked down at her body and licked his lips before glaring back in her eyes. "Or sell them."

He winked, and she gasped. His smile as he grabbed her chin in a hard grip left her with no hope of changing the man's mind. Her knees threatened to buckle underneath her, so she steeled them.

"Your padre will be happy to see you, no?" His unkind smile didn't match his words. "Now, get in the plane."

"Come on, honey." Derrick threaded his hand through hers and pulled her toward the plane. He wrapped his arm around her shoulder and whispered harshly in her ear. "What are you thinking?"

She turned to him at the bottom of the steps and traced the back of her finger down his cheek. She should've left long ago, should've hidden far away from anywhere her family could find her. He placed his hand over hers and pressed it into his cheek.

"Hasn't my family hurt you guys enough? I had to try ..." Kiki's voice cracked.

He turned his face and kissed her palm. "We're getting out of this ... together."

"Move." Matias pushed Derrick's back with a growl.

Kiki turned and walked up the stairs. Her feet weighed so much, it surprised her she could lift them. What if they couldn't get away? What if Eva never saw her parents again? Kiki's breath bottled up in her chest. Would she faint and tumble down the stairs? If she did, maybe Derrick could get Eva out of here in the chaos. He wouldn't leave Kiki, though. Not if the determined look in his eyes said anything. Kiki focused on her deep breathing she'd learned during yoga. She had to be strong so she wasn't any more of a burden to Derrick.

She stumbled as she stepped into the jet. She'd been in a lot of private planes, but this one surpassed every one of them in luxury. Leather recliners sat in front of a large plasma tv. A small table for eating or meetings was beyond the lounge chairs. A glass wall separated the TV area from a bedroom. Kiki's entire body chilled at the sight of handcuffs hanging from the headboard and different cameras waiting on a long table. She slumped onto the couch closest to the door. Her dad couldn't be involved with what that glassed bedroom suggested, could he? She shuddered as she glanced around the cabin. Opulence like this plane boasted had to cost in the hundreds of millions.

*Lord, please, please, please don't let anything happen to Eva and Derrick. Please.*

It was futile to beg to God. Evil fed off the innocent every day. What made her think her prayers were worth hearing more than any others? In fact, her family's sins stained so dark, they would taint generations.

Derrick handed Eva to Kiki and sat next to her on the couch, pulling her close. Eva's wide eyes bounced from the men coming through the door to the window. Kiki had to convince her niece it was best to lie to these men. Kiki didn't want to contemplate what they'd do to Eva and Derrick if they found out the truth.

---

Derrick stared out the window as the jet taxied down the runway. He'd screwed up again, hadn't been prepared, and now they were flying to certain death. Sure, they might not get killed right away. Yet, he'd seen the effects of human trafficking enough during his missions with the army to know that if he didn't find a way out of this, two people he cared about most in the world would die slow, torturous deaths that would draw out for years. He shuddered, his gaze darting to the bedroom on display in the back.

Why? Why had he let his guard down? Eva's sobbing ratcheted back up as the plane lurched off the runway.

"Shut your brat up!" Matias glared at them from where he stood at the table with a phone to his ear.

"Shh, Eva. It's going to be all right." Kiki held Eva tighter, rubbing her hand over Eva's head.

"I want my daddy," Eva sobbed into Kiki's neck.

Derrick glanced at the men, tension tightening his muscles. He relaxed when it appeared the men hadn't heard her soft words. Edgar and the driver were laughing at the first guy Derrick had taken out. They'd laid him in the bed where he held his head, waving obscene gestures at his friends who taunted him. Matias stared out the window as he spoke on the phone.

"Boss, we got her." Matias, who spoke in Spanish, paused and nodded his head. "Got her family too. A daughter and her lover."

He flinched, moving the phone away from his ear. Derrick's blood ran cold at the obvious upset of Matias's boss. Derrick prayed the three of them weren't stripped from each other right away.

Matias rubbed the back of his neck. "Promise, boss, this is worth it. The kid looks exactly like her, just dark-skinned."

Derrick didn't like the evil grin that stretched across Matias's face. Derrick would have to keep up the charade of being weak. Kind of hard when you're six foot four and two-hundred and twenty pounds of solid muscle, but Derrick learned real quick in the army that size didn't equate to bravery. Some of the bravest people he knew came in smaller packages.

He turned his attention to Kiki. Case in point. This five-foot nothing woman just threw herself to the wolves, giving them a very doable suggestion for not taking all of them. Though, it wouldn't have taken him hours to escape the van. More like ten minutes, thirty tops. His stomach had bottomed out when she'd stepped away from him and lied to the creep. Her eyes screamed the pain and distress she felt as she'd run her soft finger down his cheek. Her family didn't deserve to claim her as one of them. He rather liked that their captors had come to the conclusion they were a family. The thought of giving her a new name, his name, caused his skin to buzz with contentment. Maybe together they could find a way to a life healed of past mistakes and hurts.

Matias tossed the phone onto the table and fell into a chair, clicking on a soccer game. Derrick was glad the viewing choice was appropriate for Eva, though he doubted Matias cared. Eva sobbed, and Matias glared over at them.

"I want my mommy." Eva's muffled words shattered Derrick's heart and made his hands sweat.

He had to calm her down, or they'd all be screwed. He

grabbed her from Kiki and brushed her hair away from her face. He didn't know how Matias could say she looked just like Kiki. Eva resembled Sam almost down to the freckles, but maybe there was enough of Kiki's brother shining through, paired with the blue eyes that matched Kiki's, tricking someone into seeing a resemblance.

"Eva-mine, I need you to calm down, otherwise we might be in a world of trouble." Derrick hated having to be so blunt with her, but her safety depended on her cooperating.

Her eyes went wide and her lips trembled as she glanced at Kiki.

"It's going to be okay, honey." Kiki leaned over and kissed Eva's cheek. "But you need to stop crying so we can figure out how to beat these bad guys."

Eva peeked back at Matias and turned back with a glare. She sniffed, wiped her arm across her nose, and crossed her tiny arms over her chest. *That's my girl.* He almost teared up at her show of strength that was so much like her mom's.

He pulled them both close so he could whisper to them. The game on the screen would cover their conversation, but he didn't want to take the chance of being overheard. He breathed in the scent of Kiki's perfume and maple from Eva's donut at breakfast, and the combination calmed his nerves.

"Okay, ladies, here's what we're going to do." He gave them his best scheming smile.

As he explained that they'd have to pretend to be a family, he marveled at Eva's willingness to try. He wasn't sure if she could pull it off, but she'd give it her best. She laid her head on his shoulder and fell asleep. He glanced at Kiki, who stared at Eva, her eyes bright with unshed tears.

She lifted her gaze to his, and his heart pounded in his chest. If they were pretending to be a family, they better make it believable. He leaned over and pressed a soft kiss to her lips. Hers trembled beneath his. He wanted to take all her fears away, but that was impossible. So he wrapped his free arm around her and pulled her close.

# FOURTEEN

"MOMMY, WE'RE LANDING." Eva pointed out the window and turned worried eyes to Kiki.

Eva played her part perfectly, calling both Derrick and Kiki by parental nicknames. Kiki couldn't imagine the turmoil her young niece was going through. Well, maybe Kiki could since she hadn't been able to stop thinking about what kind of horrible deeds were planned for them since their abductors had grabbed them.

"It's going to be okay." So stupid. Couldn't she think of something better than that lame platitude?

More than likely, it would not be okay. More than likely, they'd end up dead or sold into slavery. How could she keep Eva from being another statistic of sex trafficking when Kiki was so inept at pretty much everything but making money? She trembled as she stared at her hands wringing in her lap. She hadn't been able to save Eva from Gregory when he'd tried to kidnap her, and Kiki certainly wouldn't be able to save Eva now.

"Hey." Derrick's large hand covered hers. "Be strong, sugar. We'll get out of this, but you need to stay calm."

She glanced at their captors as they played cards at the conference table like they hadn't just ruined lives. All her insides quaked. Could one die from extreme internal vibrations? She looked up at Derrick, pressing her lips together in fear she'd start blubbering incoherently. She couldn't show Eva how scared she was, but she also couldn't keep the fear at bay.

"I know." Derrick leaned his forehead on hers. "I'm scared too."

His calm demeanor didn't show it. She gripped his fingers in her hands. He must think she was completely pathetic. The airplane slowed, pulling Kiki's insides to her spine. Eva whimpered. Was her fascination with the window overshadowed by the unknown of what was to come next?

"Come here. I've got you." Kiki dragged Eva onto her lap.

Her niece wrapped her legs and arms around Kiki like a spider monkey. Derrick rubbed Eva's back with one hand and secured Kiki to his side with the other. The plane lurched as it contacted the ground, and Kiki's pulse thundered in her ears. She didn't want to get off of the plane.

Couldn't Derrick beat up the bad guys and steal the jet? He was a pilot. She peeked up at him. A muscle clenched in his cheek as his gaze darted from one guy to the other. Her heart kicked into overdrive at the hope of escaping. Was he thinking the same thing, figuring out a way to get them out of here? He sagged back into the couch and pulled her closer. Guess not. She squeezed her eyes shut to keep the stinging tears at bay.

She sniffed and straightened her spine. There'd be other opportunities to get free. She had a stinking special ops soldier by her side, for Pete's sake. He'd get them out of this, and she'd be ready to act when he said go.

When the plane came to a halt, Edgar walked up to them and motioned with his gun. "Let's go. Vamanos."

Derrick stood and helped Kiki stand, placing himself between her and the gun. He gave her a small smile and then, with his hand on her lower back, ushered them toward the door. The door popped as the pilot unlocked it and pushed it open.

"Welcome to Colombia." He chuckled, a cruel sound that had Kiki gulping.

The hot, thick air hit her like she'd just entered the sauna at the local spa. Eva clung tighter to Kiki, making her chest and stomach even stickier in the heat. Sweat pooled between them and ran down her stomach. She watched the steps, worried she'd trip and hurt Eva as she carried her from the plane.

"I hate the rainforest," Derrick muttered behind her.

Kiki stopped a few feet from the stairs, ignoring the men that leered at them, whispering and elbowing each other. Buildings made of cinder blocks and rusty roofing clustered past the runway, leading like a cheerless trail to an opulent beach house nestled in the jungle just past a pristine beach. A giant yacht bobbed at a dock seemingly too small to hold the large vessel.

The house wasn't huge, not even as big as their place back at the ranch, but the contrast between the cinder block structures was so sharp, Kiki swallowed in disgust. What kind of person lived in a house as beautiful as that, yet made their lackeys live in squalor? Or were the cinder block buildings for something else? She shivered despite the stifling heat.

What looked like a roof to a large building peeked out of

the jungle behind the cluster of buildings. Handfuls of men meandered or loitered here and there. Only the group by the plane gave the new arrivals any notice. Just how often did this place get fresh captives?

"Take them to the row." Matias's quick Spanish was hard for her to follow as he motioned to Edgar. "I'm going to see the boss."

The stench of unwashed bodies and rotting vegetation wafted over her as she followed Edgar past the men still ogling. She stifled the urge to hold her nose. Instead, she leaned her head closer to Eva's, inhaling her sweet scent. Derrick stepped up next to her and wrapped his arm around her lower back. The action gave her the strength to walk tall and not react when the men whistled and bantered between themselves.

They followed Edgar to a long, single story building with at least eight rusty red doors interrupting the gray face like an old-time motel. This structure wasn't inviting, though. It exuded foreboding, like if they stepped through a doorway, they'd never come back out. As they got closer, more insidious details separated from the dreary facade. Large padlocks hung from each entryway, and what looked like a long window covering with a handle on it graced each door at the bottom. It was the perfect size to pass a tray of food inside like they did in some prisons.

Kiki's muscles weakened, and she adjusted her grip on Eva. Could Derrick knock out Edgar so they could dash into the jungle and escape? She turned her head to whisper to Derrick when a man stepped out of the shadows of the building, a machine gun held loosely in his hands as his gaze bounced between Kiki and Derrick. He shifted the toothpick held in his mouth from one side to the other. His eyes weren't hard like the other men there, more assessing with a slight look of surprise when his gaze settled on Derrick.

Kiki shook her head and focused on the door Edgar stopped in front of. It didn't matter what the man with the gun looked like. His presence squashed her escape plans, at least for the moment.

The door opened with a loud scrape of metal against cement. A shiver skittered up her spine and into her hair like a bunch of cockroaches racing along her skin. She stepped backward, her body revolting against the dark space revealed within. Edgar sneered and barked a laugh.

*Be strong, Kiki. Don't react.*

Derrick rubbed his hand up and down her arm. Thank God that Derrick was here with her. What a horrible thought! Oh, that Matias would have left Derrick and Eva behind in the van. At least then they'd be safe, though Kiki doubted she'd be keeping it together if Derrick wasn't holding her up.

"Your room, my friends." Edgar bowed with a snicker as he extended his arm through the door.

She sniffed, put on her best spoiled rich girl facade she'd perfected in private school, and stomped past Edgar. What she wouldn't give to slam the heel of her palm into his smug chin. She stifled the urge by holding tighter to Eva. The last thing Kiki wanted to do was to provoke the man and make their time here worse.

She skidded to a halt in the middle of the room. Four cinder block walls about ten feet long closed in around her. The only light shone weakly from a tiny barred window high on the opposite wall from the door. The barren space held a filthy double mattress thrown onto the cement floor, a clear jug of water, and a bucket in the corner that had streaks of brown on the inside and flies darting in and out.

Kiki closed her eyes and swallowed the vomit that hit her throat. The door slammed shut with another laugh from Edgar. Kiki flinched, and Eva sobbed as she buried her face into Kiki's neck. *God, why?* Why was this happening?

Who was she fooling? Her father was somehow behind this latest disaster. Would her family ever stop hurting other people? Would she ever get away from the chaos and despair they created?

Derrick pulled Kiki into a tight hug, squishing a crying Eva between them. A sob ripped through Kiki, almost choking her as she swallowed it down. Another quickly followed. Derrick took Eva from Kiki's arms and wrapped his arm even tighter around Kiki's back. She gripped the hem of his shirt in her fists as sob after sob broke loose from her thin control.

# FIFTEEN

"WE NEED to take stock of our situation." Derrick's throat scratched as he swallowed and squeezed Kiki closer.

*Then let her go, numskull.*

He couldn't though. The need to hold her tight, to feel that she was okay, burned almost as hot as the need to figure out how to get out of the hell they were in. Holding her wouldn't help them, so he kissed her temple and set Eva on the disgusting mattress, trying not to think about what might be crawling on it.

"Okay, Eva-mine, we need to search for a way out and gather our resources, like a good soldier does in every situation." He silently thanked God for Eva's adventurous spirit and her love of playing pretend. How many of their "secret missions" they'd had back at the ranch, spying or rescuing the fair maiden, had helped prepare her for this?

"Yes, sir." Eva's lips trembled, and her salute didn't hold its usual fervor.

"Okay, search the room for anything we can use. I'll check the window."

Derrick stomped to the opening and tested the bars. Solid. No worries. Loose bars were a pipe dream, anyway.

He pulled himself up to scan what was outside. A wall lined one side of a dirt yard. Embedded in the wall were hooks and loops like where prisoners were tied. On the other side of the yard was a covered sitting area with cushioned chairs, tables, and a bar. An auction house?

He pushed the anger down, not wanting emotion to override what he needed to accomplish. Beyond the small yard, the jungle waited. No fencing that he could see separated them from escape, so when he could figure out how to get them out of this cell—he refused to think of it as anything but that—then they could flee through the rainforest. He could keep them alive for weeks in the lush trees until they made it to safety.

"What's out there?" Kiki stepped up beside him and touched his arm.

"Not much."

He put his feet back on the ground and brushed off his hands, afraid to look her in the eye. She'd see the lie. He didn't want her knowing the depth of evil they'd found themselves in.

She poked her finger into his bicep. "Don't coddle me. That won't help."

She pushed between him and the wall and, before he could react, pulled herself up to look through the window. Her arms shook, so he grabbed her waist to hold her up. She was so small, barely bigger than a child. Could he keep her safe? He took a deep breath and leaned his forehead on her back.

She sucked in and let go of the bars. He didn't want to let her go, so when her feet touched the ground, he kept his hands on her waist. She turned in his hands and placed her palms on his chest.

"Is that—" Her voice caught, and he nodded.

"What is it? I want to see." Eva stepped up, grabbing Derrick's hand.

"The jungle, pumpkin. Here, let me show you." Kiki slid out from Derrick's grasp and lifted Eva up to the window.

What was she doing? Eva was sure to see the wall and ask. He didn't want to have to explain that to her. He rubbed his hand over his prickly head, missing the smoothly shaved feel he usually had.

"See the big leaves, trees, and those pretty red flowers?" Kiki asked as she lowered Eva.

Eva nodded. "Yeah."

"We get in there, and Uncle D will help us disappear." Kiki smiled like the thought excited her, and this was a big game. "We'll get to smear mud all over ourselves and stick leaves in our hair and clothes so we blend in to our surroundings and trick these jerks."

Derrick snorted. With his and Eva's dark skin, Kiki was the only one who would need to smear herself with mud. He couldn't squash Eva's excitement, though.

She jumped up and down, clapping her hands. "I love hide and seek."

"Me too." Kiki peeked at Derrick, a spark of worry crossing her face before she shuttered it and turned back to Eva. "I need you to push on these blocks that are low. We need to see if we can find any that are loose."

Eva saluted and got busy pushing on blocks. Kiki strode over to the mattress and bent down to it. Derrick followed, shaking off his amazement of Kiki's ability to turn this captivity into a game.

Kiki pulled at the mattress edge. "There's a wire in here. Could we somehow get it out and use it as a weapon or something?"

"Good idea." He would've come up with the same plan, and that she thought of the same thing impressed him. It was obvious no one else who'd been captured had.

"I'm just not strong enough to rip the fabric. That's probably why it's still in there." Kiki shuddered and pushed a shaking hand through her bobbed hair.

He gripped the mattress and pulled. For a ratty thing, its seams still held their strength. He lifted his shirt and touched his fake scar on his back. His preparedness for trouble didn't seem such overkill now as it did the day before. He picked at the edge of the scar and peeled it up.

Kiki gasped, her fingers skimming his skin, shooting tingles up his back. "What?"

"It's my escape kit." He shrugged as he laid the fake silicone scar on the mattress. "Habit from my time in the army."

Would she think he was crazy? What kind of person still glued razor blades and handcuff keys to their body after being out of the military for two years? It didn't matter. His kit might just save their lives.

"Genius." Kiki grabbed the scar that still had the blade and key glued to it and turned it over in her hands. "Amazing." She turned to him. "You're amazing."

She leaned in and kissed his lips. Though her touch fluttered soft and tentative against his mouth, it sent warmth and determination coursing through him. He had to get her and Eva out of this, no matter the cost.

She leaned her forehead on his. "I'm a horrible person ... I'm glad you're here with me."

Her words exploded his resolve to keep their relationship as friends to smithereens. He would figure things out, maybe purchase a ranch close to the Stryker place. Maybe him staying would be better after all. He gripped her fingers and brought her hand to his lips. He held her gaze, her eyes widening, as he pressed his mouth to the inside of her wrist.

"We're getting out of this, and when we do, I don't want us to waste any more time circling each other. Understand?"

She gulped, her gaze darting to his lips before she nodded slowly.

His mouth tipped in a one-sided smile before he schooled it. His words would give them both something to look forward to. First, though, he had to escape.

"Aunt Kiki, I found something," Eva whispered from the corner.

Derrick jerked from Kiki and crossed to Eva. He pushed his worry aside and tucked it away. He needed to focus. Every minute he wasted was a minute that could've got them free.

Eva beamed at him and pointed to a low brick. This little girl was amazing, so much stronger than he'd ever imagined. He bent to the brick and pushed. It wiggled, but just a little. They'd have to remove a lot of bricks for him to squeeze through the hole, but if they got two loose, at least Kiki and Eva could run. Lessons in jungle survival would begin immediately.

Ripping pulled his attention to the bed where Kiki sliced the edge of the mattress and yanked the wire out of the fabric. Her focused expression galvanized his resolve. He'd get them out of this cell, even if he had to tear the bricks loose with his bare hands. Then he'd get himself free.

If he didn't have to worry about Kiki and Eva, he could escape much easier. He pushed his shoulders back, a plan forming in his head. Doubt had no space in his thoughts if he was going to get his family free.

# SIXTEEN

KIKI SAT on the edge of the mattress, relishing the soft snores of a little girl curled on the far side of the bed. Eva had helped Kiki strip the wire and fabric that had covered it. They'd braided the fabric into a long cord that they wrapped through Eva's belt loops. When they'd finished that, Eva had collapsed onto the mattress with a sigh, her eyelids fighting a losing battle with sleep, while Derrick scraped away at the mortar around the loose block with a tool he'd fashioned out of some wire.

Kiki flexed her fingers, stiff from feeding a length of the mattress wire along the wire already in her bra. After Derrick had hidden the razor in her shoe and the handcuff key in the hem of her shorts, he told her to hide the wire in her bra. Apparently, special ops members liked to conceal all kinds of useful tools in their clothing and on their body.

She'd balked at taking the razor and key. Would she even know how to use them? Derrick had insisted and shown her his other scar that held the same tools.

She shook her head and smirked as she finished pushing the rest of the wire through. He proved more industrious than she'd imagined. She pulled her arms into her tank top and put on her redesigned bra. It pushed uncomfortably against her skin. She shifted it before giving up with a huff. It definitely wouldn't win any designer awards.

The sun had gone down a few hours before, and Kiki had struggled with pushing down the panic that darkness brought. Shortly after the colors faded from the sky, a full moon rose above the treetops, bathing the small space in a pale light that eased her building fears. It was silly, really. What grown woman was afraid of the dark?

Okay, so the newest circumstances had ramped that deeply hidden fear to the top of her subconscious. All the scary movies her friends had forced her to watch growing up bubbled to the surface of her memory, combining all those horrors that had given her nightmares for years with the new terror that two people she loved would have to endure them. She wrapped her arms around her belly, her skin clammy with the panic building in her.

Derrick's arm jerked, and a hiss filled the air, pulling her thoughts from the selfish spiral they'd been heading down. Kiki stood and crossed the few steps to Derrick. His motions were slow, like he was tired out. It wasn't like they'd probably be here long enough to escape through the opening, especially since they'd need to scrape several loose for Derrick to fit through. He didn't need to exhaust himself on a pointless endeavor.

She touched his arm to stop him. "Let me see."

He pulled away. "I'm fine."

She rolled her eyes. "Derrick, please. Eva's asleep. You can stop pretending to get us an escape route. You need to save your strength for when we escape." She laid her hand on his, hoping he'd stop.

"If I can push this out, you and Eva could get to the

jungle." He shook his hand free, and, with renewed vigor, rubbed the wire against the wall.

He wasn't planning on going with them? Her blood froze as she balled her trembling hand into a fist. Is that why he'd been drilling them on jungle survival? She couldn't make it without him, especially with a kid in tow.

"What are you saying?" she hissed at him, not caring that her worry came out as an angry tone.

"I'm getting you out of here." Derrick's cheek muscle flexed in the pale light. "Besides, I can escape easier if it's just me."

She flinched. Of course he could. Why was she always so selfish, only thinking about herself? Was it a family trait so engrained in her DNA that she'd never break free from it? Her father and mother certainly were. She'd known from an early age that her brother was completely self-absorbed. She'd tried so hard to be different, to be someone others would like, but it seemed there was no getting away from the egotistical Payne genes.

She stood and took two jerky steps back. "I'm sorry."

She pushed her fingers through her hair and pulled to focus on something other than the tears stinging her eyes and the weightiness in her chest. When that didn't help, she squeezed her eyes shut. She couldn't look at her niece curled up on the disgusting mattress—couldn't look at the slump of Derrick's shoulders as he scraped for a freedom he couldn't join them in. Why had she ever thought she could dodge her family's sins?

"Hey." Derrick's rough hands rubbed down her arms.

"I'm sorry. I'm so sorry I keep bringing trouble your way." She buried her face in her palms, her stomach twisting with guilt.

"This isn't your fault." His hands stilled on her arms.

"It is. I should've never stayed. I should've never thought a Payne would be good for Eva. Good for anyone." Her disgust with herself compounded with the guilt, and she stepped back to put some space between them.

"Don't say that." He tightened his grip on her biceps.

Kiki twisted her arms and broke his hold, not caring that her anguish wet her cheeks. "I can't ever get away from what my parents have done ... what I was a part of."

"You didn't know what they were up to." He reached for her, and she pulled her arm out of reach. How could he possibly want to be with her when she was so naive?

"That makes me even worse." She crossed her arms, hugging herself as the pain she'd struggled to get over rushed back to the surface. "All the signs were there. I should've known."

He snaked his arm around her back before she could move away. His thumb skated across her cheek, drying her tears. If only she could allow his earlier declaration to come true. The more she thought about it, though, the more she realized she couldn't let anything develop. If they ever got out of this mess, she'd run as far from the ranch as she could, taking the pain of her family with her.

"Oh, sugar, stop blaming yourself. You aren't them." Derrick's rough voice closed her throat as she stifled her whimpers down.

"That's just it. I'm still the selfish person I always was." Kiki pushed on his chest.

"No, you aren't." Derrick pulled her close, his hands spreading heat across her back. "You are the most unselfish person I know."

She shook her head.

"Who else would endure hours and hours of movies they hate without saying a word?"

"I just liked being around y'all."

"Who else takes on extra work to help a friend make money, for nothing in return?"

Her muscles relaxed as he speared his fingers into her hair.

"That was a fair trade," she whispered.

"Who else will drop everything to watch her niece, even though they have a lot to do?"

"Every single one of you." She turned her head to look at the slight form on the mattress. "Lot of good that did. She might never see her parents again, and it's all my fault."

"It's not. It's these men's fault, maybe your father's, but not yours." Derrick cupped both his hands on her neck and forced her to look at him. "I've watched you. From the moment you came bloodied and bruised to the ranch, I've seen who you are inside." His voice dropped lower. "You're brave and caring. You have one of the most tender hearts I've ever witnessed. You're strong, and I saw the joy you found in Eva and our family."

His words planted hope in her chest and made her light-headed. He claimed her mouth softly, heating her already warm body to boiling. She grabbed his forearms to steady herself as he kissed a trail to her ear. Could what he said be true? She should think about it, ask him what he meant, but all thought evaporated from her brain but him.

His breath blew hot against her earlobe, sending shivers down her back. "You're amazing, Kiki. I think I might be losing my heart to you."

He captured her lips with a desperation that rivaled her own. Could this amazing man love her? It couldn't be true, but the soft moan he sounded and how he gently pulled her tighter to him said it was.

She dragged her mouth from his, amazed to find her

arms wrapped around him. She peered into his face, seeing the truth of his words in his eyes. She swallowed down the overwhelming joy that threatened to choke her with unshed tears.

"I don't want to lose you." Her voice was tight as it pushed past her emotions. She buried her face into his shirt. "But I'm so scared. What if we never get free? I can't watch you and Eva suffer, knowing it's because of me."

"Shh." He curved his body around hers, wrapping her in his protection. "We're going to figure this out. I promise. Remember, I'm good at this, really good."

She sniffed and nodded against his chest. He was right. Maybe this wouldn't end in her witnessing her loved ones die. Eva whimpered in her sleep on the mattress.

"Come on. Let's get some shuteye." Derrick kissed Kiki one last time, then led her to the bed.

When she scooted to the middle, Eva rolled over and snuggled against Kiki's chest. Fear tried to bubble its way back to the top of her thoughts, but she pushed it down. She wrapped her arms around Eva, determined to do everything she could to keep her niece safe. The mattress dipped, and Derrick curled up against her back, wrapping his arm around both her and Eva. Kiki closed her eyes and breathed out. Together, they'd all escape. She lifted that thought up in prayer as she drifted to sleep.

# SEVENTEEN

THE BIRDS SQUAWKED in the jungle, signaling the start of a new day. Derrick took a deep breath, not wanting to move from where he held Kiki and Eva. What was he thinking, telling her she held his heart? He'd barely held in telling her the entire truth and declaring his love like some sappy movie. Talk about jumping into a relationship full steam.

His lips twitched up with the memory of her saying she didn't want to lose him. When they got out of this mess, he wasn't wasting any more time. A monkey shrieked outside, sending a shiver down his spine, and the rest of what she'd said slammed into his brain, cooling his hope. He had to get them out first.

He had to stay alert.

Think through every contingency.

Be ready to attack when the opportunity arose, otherwise they'd all just become another statistic of the Colombian crime ring. He took one more breath of Kiki, infusing himself with purpose, and carefully lifted his arm from around those he'd risk anything for.

He sat up and stared at the two snuggled together. How had Kiki slept with Eva's arm wrapped around the back of her neck like it was? Eva's mouth hung open as she softly snored.

Would this be his and Kiki's future? Her tanned arms holding their children while they slept? He hungered for that more than he'd ever wanted anything. Would she give up the guilt she felt for her family's corruption?

*Son, you can't keep blaming yourself for Josiah's death. No one's condemning you for that mistake, bud.*

Derrick shook his head as his father's words from the last time Derrick had visited replayed in his ears. Could he help show her that any blame she held was forgiven? Could he share his own past to help heal her future?

*Your mom and I want you to be free of this burden, to live your life for yourself rather than what you think Josiah would've done.*

The sun shone through the high window, heating Derrick's already sticky skin. He'd tried to convince his dad that wasn't what he was doing, that his need to always be prepared had nothing to do with failing Josiah. The conversation was more to convince himself than his father.

*It's just, I pray you find peace, peace with yourself and peace in God.*

The heat spread through him, searing all the way to his fingers and toes. Why was he thinking about this now? His heart hammered in his chest and goosebumps covered his skin, though humidity hung thick and stifling in the air. He wanted that peace his father talked about, that God had promised. Derrick hung his head. He yearned for it, had thought if he prepared enough, he'd find it. He snorted. How thick could he be?

"Okay, I relent," he whispered.

He raised his head with a smile as serenity settled over him like cool water. Kiki's forehead scrunched, and she shifted on the bed. He prayed for help, prayed that God would save her and Eva, even if it meant Derrick had to die.

*Do not let your hearts be troubled and do not be afraid.*

His pulse roared in his ears. That sounded ominous. Footsteps approached, and he quickly scanned the room to make sure they'd hidden their work.

"Kiki, wake up, sugar." Derrick bent down and shook her shoulder.

Her eyes popped open, and her breath sucked in. "What's happening?"

"Someone's coming."

Her eyes widened even further before she turned to Eva and gently woke her. Derrick stood just as a clicking of the lock sounded through the door. Kiki scrambled to her feet, pulling Eva with her and tucking the child against the wall. Already Kiki's muscles bunched as if in preparation of what would come.

"Remember what I told you." Derrick held his hand up in a calming motion like he did with his frightened horses.

Kiki nodded, but the color drained from her tanned skin. The scrape of the metal door against the concrete floor turned his focus forward. Edgar stepped into the space, a triumphant smile stretched across his face. The guard with the gun stood in the doorway behind Edgar, his face blank of expression.

"How was your night? Comfy? Did you sleep well?" His sadistic smile grew with each question. "I hate to tell you that your accommodations are about to be downgraded. Well, for one of you, that is."

No. Derrick's hands fisted. They couldn't get separated.

"The thing is, not all buyers want scrawny girls. And

you, amigo, will bring a good price, even if you have to be drugged." Edgar scanned up and down Derrick's body and wiped a filthy hand across his mouth.

Derrick's stomach revolted in disgust, and he sneered. Edgar's arm swung quick, connecting with Derrick's temple and buckling his knees with the sudden pain. Eva's screams echoed in his head as he shook away the stars that swam in front of his eyes. Rustling behind him turned his gaze to where Edgar pointed a gun at Kiki, who hid Eva's face in her neck.

"You go nicely with Marco or I will hurt them." Edgar smiled again, his thick accent faking charm. "I'm not so picky about my conquests—guapo men, skinny girls, or too-short women." He shrugged. "Torture is torture, and it turns me on."

Derrick held up one hand in surrender as he pushed himself off the ground with the other and stood. "I'm going. Just don't hurt them, please."

Kiki's eyes bulged without blinking. She pressed her lips tight and shook her head. Derrick held her gaze, willing her to be strong.

"No!" Eva shrieked, her arms exploding from around Kiki's neck to smack Edgar's face. "Leave him alone!"

Kiki grabbed Eva's arms and held her struggling form. "Eva, sweetie, *shh*. Calm down." Kiki turned her back to Edgar and moved to the corner of the room under the window.

Edgar pressed his fingers to his cheek where Eva had hit him. "A wildcat. How fun." He motioned to Marco. "Go."

Marco grabbed Derrick's arm, his grip tight but not unbreakable. Derrick stole one last look at Kiki where she watched him leave. Her lips trembled and eyes glistened with unshed tears. Edgar stepped between them, blocking her from Derrick's view, and followed him out.

Derrick breathed easier as Edgar slammed the door closed and clicked the lock with a testing shake. He wouldn't be hurting Kiki or Eva, at least not now. Derrick turned forward and scanned his surroundings as Marco led him around the building to the backyard. Could he break Marco's hold and make it to the jungle?

"Listen quick, Sergeant Nicholson." Marco's harsh whisper stopped Derrick's scheming as he peeked to the man beside him. "Vega, CIA. I can't break my cover, but I'll help how I can."

Derrick bobbed his head as he hung it in mock defeat.

"I'll get your women on the yacht. There's a garage for the watercraft, stern-starboard side, you can access by swimming."

Derrick had boarded yachts in other rescue missions in a similar way. Relief loosened his limbs that his chance at saving them was a familiar one. Marco led Derrick to the wall outside the window. So, they would chain him.

"We hold prisoners on the port quarter, second level." Marco slapped handcuffs on Derrick's wrists. "You have until tomorrow." His words held urgency.

"How do you like your new home?" Edgar yelled from the corner of the building where he stood with his gun at the ready.

Derrick glared. "I've had better."

Edgar laughed, his head tipping back like Derrick had just told the world's funniest joke. "I like you. You've got, how do you Americans say ...? Spunk."

Marco looped a chain around the handcuffs and locked it so Derrick's hands were stretched over his head. The spy peeked at something to the right of Derrick's head and, with a quick nod that way, struck Derrick across the cheek with a blow that left his ears ringing.

"You've got thirty minutes." Marco's hoarse voice barely came through the fog in his ears.

Marco adjusted himself and hollered in Spanish at Edgar about the burly American being nothing but a weakling. Derrick rotated his jaw as he slumped against the wall. The CIA sure didn't pull their punches. He glanced to where Marco had indicated. Gratitude flooded in as a satisfied smile twitched Derrick's lips up.

# EIGHTEEN

"D!" Eva thrashed hard in Kiki's arms.

Kiki put Eva down, not wanting to drop her. Stumbling, Eva dashed to the door and pounded her tiny fists on the metal. Her cries echoed Kiki's own despair. Were they really going to sell Derrick? No, he'd get free, somehow.

Edgar's taunting voice floated through the window, followed by Derrick's calm tone. Kiki stretched on her toes to grab the bars and pulled herself up. Derrick's hands extended high above his head, chained to that horrible wall. Marco swung, knocking Derrick's head sideways, and Kiki gasped at the unnecessary violence.

"I can't wait to see you strung up, Señorita Payne." Edgar spoke right below the other side of the window. "What a thrilling picture that will be."

Kiki shuddered, lowered herself to the floor, and leaned against the wall. The rough surface scratched against her forehead. She wished she could come back with some witty remark, but her brain froze with the image of Eva chained to that wall.

Was that their fate? Would an innocent girl be auctioned off to the highest bidder? Though only five, Eva was beautiful with her rose-toned brown skin, freckled liberally across her nose and cheeks, and her bright blue eyes. Kiki's stomach rolled at what would happen to her niece if Kiki fell apart like she wanted.

Eva's pounding had lost its strength, her sobs filling the small room with the heavy weight of fear and heartbreak. Kiki pushed away from the wall and moved to Eva, scooping her up and taking her to the window. The little girl's tears soaked Kiki's neck, running down her skin, and her tiny fingers dug into Kiki's skin where they clung to her.

"Eva, honey. Derrick's all right. He's right outside. I'm going to lift you up to let you see, but you have to remember what we told you. These guys think we're a family. Okay?"

Eva nodded, her sad eyes wide as she lifted her head. Was it a mistake to show her Derrick? Probably, but maybe if she knew Derrick was relatively safe, she'd calm down. Kiki's arms burned as she lifted Eva to the window.

"Daddy!" Eva yelled, her voice shrill with emotion, the instant her face cleared the window.

"Eva? Eva, honey, I'm fine." Derrick's firm voice soothed over Kiki's tight nerves and infused her with strength.

"Daddy, I'm scared."

"I know, honey. You and mommy be brave for me okay, Eva-mine?" Derrick's voice strained, and Kiki imagined having his arms bound like that had to hurt.

Kiki's own arms burned with the effort of keeping Eva held up. "Eva, my arms can't hold you anymore. Tell him we love him."

"We love you, Daddy. We'll be strong."

"I love you too, Eva—you and Mommy." Derrick's voice held a hint of emotion Kiki couldn't place.

Eva blew a kiss and sighed as Kiki lowered her to the floor. "Why was Uncle D's arm bleeding?"

Bleeding? Kiki didn't remember seeing any blood. Of course, Marco slamming his fist into Derrick's face had distracted her.

"I don't know, honey, but he'll be okay." Kiki crouched down and pulled Eva into a hug. "A little scratch won't get him down."

Footsteps approached outside, and Kiki tensed. Eva trembled as she turned her gaze to the door. What terror did these sickos have planned now? The small slot opened at the bottom of the door, and a tray slid in, followed by a canteen.

"Breakfast," a gruff voice said before the little opening snapped shut.

Eva's nose wrinkled at the greasy beans and rice filling the chipped bowl. "Beans for breakfast?"

Kiki forced a smile. "I love beans, and look, they even gave us tortillas. How'd they know burritos are one of my favorites?"

Kiki hugged Eva, then stepped to the tray. Grease congealed along the edge of the bowl. Kiki bit her lip, then schooled her expression. She stirred the food, picked the tray up, and took it to the bed.

"Breakfast in bed." Kiki put as much cheer as she could into her voice. "Just like princesses have."

Maybe bringing up Eva's obsession would distract her from the different meal. Her lips trembled into a slight smile. Well, maybe it wouldn't work, but at least eating gave them something to do.

"It looks like there might be some pork in here." Kiki at

least hoped it was pork as she stirred the concoction again and spooned some onto a tortilla.

After folding it, she stretched it out to Eva. She shook her head and backed up like Kiki held out a snake instead of food. She pulled her hand back and looked at the burrito. Yeah, Kiki probably should test it first. She swallowed hard, then took a tentative bite. While seasonings didn't explode into her mouth, the bland food wasn't disgusting— just flavorless. She took another bite, then held it up for Eva.

"It's not bad, just doesn't have Sosimo's flare." Kiki waved Eva forward. "Come on, honey. You have to eat if we want to stay healthy and escape."

Eva took one step forward, her shoulders hunched in, diminishing her already tiny frame. If only Kiki could fix this, could get Eva free. They'd escape this hell somehow. Hadn't Kiki been training the last several months for this? Hadn't she been pushing herself to not be the weak person she had been?

Kiki didn't think Derrick had been lying when he'd said she'd impressed him. She would've gotten away from their abductors if Matias hadn't pushed that gun to Eva's head. If Kiki stayed alert, at the ready for an opportunity, she would get them free. Then, she'd use all that info Derrick had drilled in her the last day to survive in the jungle until she could find help.

Eva took a bite from Kiki's hand, her nervous expression shifting to exasperation. "These guys need to spice things up. Maybe after Daddy and the others come and kick their backsides and rescue us, Sosimo can teach them how to cook."

Kiki snorted as Eva took the burrito and plopped down on the mattress. Oh, to think like a five-year-old again, where the world's problems were answered so simply. Kiki had no illusions of a grand rescue, not with how far they'd been taken. Yet she also wasn't willing to roll over and die. She'd get them free one way or another, then she'd figure out how to get them home. She slapped the spoon of beans onto her tortilla with extra force as determination burned hot within her.

# NINETEEN

METAL from the handcuffs bit into Derrick's skin as he jammed the empty hook protruding from the wall back into the open space of the restraint. With the cuff pushed up on his forearm as far as it would go, he leaned his weight so that the hook bent the restraint. He gritted his teeth as the jagged metal sliced into his skin. The cuff snapped, flooding adrenaline through his body as his arms came free.

He glanced around for any enemy while he twisted his wrist and dashed for the jungle. He stole one last look back, his throat tightening at the memory of Eva hollering out the window. Her tiny fingers wrapped around the bars and face pressed against them had nearly torn his heart in two. Now, he had to leave them unprotected. He just prayed Marco had told the truth. If whatever was happening went down the next day, that gave Derrick plenty of time to plan. He just had to stay out of sight. He ducked into the rainforest, pushing the large leaves out of the way.

This place would explode like an angry wasps' nest the minute they discovered he had escaped. He needed to find a place to lie low until the darkness of night covered his actions. The outline of a building peeked through the thick leaves. Derrick slowed, ducking into a dense bush to survey the area.

He pushed a branch down and peered through the foliage. Though birds and monkeys made a raucous clatter in the treetops, he detected no humans roaming the dirt path that stretched to other buildings poking out of the trees farther down. He turned to the structure in front of him. Maybe he could find a place to hide inside. Something about the building looked familiar, so he leaned farther out of the brush to get a closer look. The door he had breached with Ethan and Rafe on that mission that changed his life forever stood not ten feet from him once again.

Derrick's head spun, and he stumbled back, his knee dropping to the ground. His heart pounded hard and fast against his ribs like a M240 machine gun. It couldn't be. Derrick shook his head, rubbing his scalp with his palm. He had to be mistaken.

He pushed the branches aside again, his hand shaking the leaves with his trembling. He had to make sure he wasn't imagining things. He'd never forget the pitted cement at the base of the barn walls or the metal extension jutting from the far side of the original building. He'd never forget the look on Ethan's face as he turned from the doorway, two bullet holes bleeding from his chest. The door still had holes from the rounds that had punched into it as the entire complex had barreled down on Derrick and his team.

He swallowed the acid burning up his throat. Were there women and children in the metal addition right now, waiting to be auctioned? Sosimo had found that doozy out when Colonel Johnson had tried to steal June's invention the fall before. Derrick and his team's mission to rescue the Isaacs had been sabotaged from the start. With the Eyes Beyond tech hidden before the mission, his team hadn't seen the shapes of the hostages being held just twenty feet away. Otherwise, they would've come back with an army and stormed the complex.

He shook his head again to clear it of the memories. He couldn't dwell on that now. He had to hide. He froze, a slow smile building on his face. He had studied the map surrounding this area for that mission. Their extraction point had been along a river.

He took off through the woods toward the old rendezvous. If he could get to the river, leaving a trail along the way, he could circle back. If his ruse worked and they took time to track him, he'd decrease the number of men hanging out at the complex.

A shout far behind him and the metal peal of a bell warned him the chase was on. He stretched his legs wider as he ran in the direction they'd escaped two years before. He could almost feel the weight of his best friend slung over his shoulder. The way Ethan's body had flopped against Derrick's back still gave him nightmares.

A branch whacked him in the face, forcing his attention to the surrounding jungle. Ethan Stryker was dead, and there had been nothing Derrick could do to save him. Kiki and Eva needed him to execute their rescue, and he couldn't do that with his focus divided.

He stepped in a mud puddle, making sure his foot slid to give the illusion of haste. Half a klick later, he stumbled into a bush and broke several branches. Shouting filtered through the jungle behind him as he scanned the forest for anyone hiding.

He skidded as the jungle opened up to the clearing before the river. On the opposite side of the river, a rock-faced cliff lined both sides of a path that continued through the foliage. He sprinted to the river's edge and waded into the warm water. As murkiness twisted around his legs, he scanned the banks in front and behind him.

He stepped from the river close to the rock cliff. Pressing his foot hard into the mud, he took several steps to the dry dirt and turned into the jungle. Then, with careful movement, he backtracked into his footsteps until he reached the rocks.

He peered up the height of the cliff. The rocks bent as his head spun. While he'd had to climb during his time in the army, it always filled him with a dread he couldn't force down. He wiped his sweaty hand on his shirt, praying they wouldn't get so slick he'd slip to his death. Reaching as high as he could, he gripped the rough surface and pulled himself up the cliff.

Yells grew closer as birds took off from the trees on the opposite side of the river. He didn't have much time. His breathing rasped loud in his ears. He kept his feet off the rocks until he was several yards above the ground. Hopefully, no one would see any prints that high.

He scrambled higher, his heart jumping into his throat when his hands, slick with sweat and muddy river water, slipped. Darker shadows moved within the jungle on the opposite side. He glanced up. Only a few feet more.

His arms burned as he reached higher, pushing his feet against the rocks. A stone broke loose from under his foot and tumbled down the cliff. Derrick's heart faltered as the memory of Josiah's terror-filled yell saturated his mind. He shook the image loose and glanced at the rocks on the path. Hopefully, his pursuers wouldn't notice the new debris on the path.

"¡De prisa!" Edgar's command to hurry pushed Derrick

over the top just as Edgar rushed from the jungle across the expanse.

Derrick pressed himself flat against the ground, holding perfectly still. Closing his eyes, he relaxed into the ground. As he let the tall grass that covered the flat, treeless top of the cliff hide him, he caught his breath. Splashing of the men reached him just as the weight of something shifted onto his foot.

He squeezed his eyes shut, willing his body not to react as the creature slithered up his leg, its body wrapping tightly around his calf. Exclamations of the men on the hunt bounced up the walls as they raced into the jungle. The breath he'd held whooshed out, and he reached down to pry the boa loose. His body convulsed in a shiver as he set the offending snake aside.

Derrick belly crawled through the grass until he reached the cover of the trees, laying out his mission in his head. He had to work his way back to the complex before dark. Otherwise, he couldn't put the next part of his plan into action, couldn't save the woman he was pretty sure he would spend the rest of his life with if only he didn't fail ... again.

# TWENTY

"WHAT IF WE SEE A BRIGHT, pretty frog or snake?" Kiki tossed the pebble onto the hopscotch she and Eva had marked on the cement and jumped across the game.

"Don't touch, even if it's super cute." Eva scrunched up her nose. "If we can't fish, where do we find food?"

"We find some grub under a log." Kiki tickled Eva's belly. "Wonder if the bugs will wiggle in our tummies?"

Eva's giggle as she twisted away pushed against the shadows of despair that had threatened to close in around Kiki since realizing Derrick had escaped. She kept reminding herself that it was a good thing he was no longer chained to the wall, but her worry kept sliding its icy fingers along her skin—worry for Derrick's safety and worry he'd never return. That last was uncalled for, and she told herself that repeatedly. Derrick would never abandon her and Eva, even if it cost him his life.

"How do we get water?" Kiki peppered the next question in the quiz game they'd been playing all afternoon.

"Rain in the can-tain," Eva sang, making canteen rhyme.

She threw her hands up in the air and jumped and twirled like she was dancing in the rain. Kiki bounced up beside her and joined in. It was easy to stay upbeat with the little darling there. Kiki tried not to think about the faceless women and children that had been held in the room before them, fearfully waiting a horrible fate.

Kiki's own fear still simmered in her gut. Having Eva to focus on made Kiki keep the heat of her terror from boiling over. The silly rainforest survival trivia and hopscotch kept her brain alert. She'd have to ask Derrick if soldiers ever did anything like that to keep their minds focused.

She had a lot of things she'd have to ask Derrick about when all this was done.

Like if he meant it when he told Eva that he loved Mommy.

Or if he still wanted to see where things between them went.

Leaning against the cinderblock wall under the window, Kiki took in a deep breath. That last question pinched at her heart. Leaving still felt like the right thing to do. If she disappeared from Derrick, Eva, and the others' lives, her father's so-called associates would no longer be a threat. If she made a large enough trail in the leaving, going underground only after it was apparent she no longer lived at the Silver Wolf Ranch, Sam and Zeke could stop being on guard all the time.

Eva flopped on to the bed with an exaggerated sigh. "I love dancing in the rain."

"Me too, nugget." Kiki smiled as her chest grew tight.

She'd miss her family, miss the love she'd found at the ranch. Making sure Eva made it home and stayed safe was what was important now. Nothing else mattered but that. Not anymore.

"Do you think we'll get something other than cold beans and tortillas for dinner tonight?" Eva brought her hands to rest over her stomach.

"I'm not sure."

"We might have to pretend we're having a tea party or something." Eva sat up quickly, her eyes wide with excitement. "Oh ... maybe we can pretend we're Alice in Wonderland. Maybe the beans will let me grow huge like Alice did, and I'll bust us out of this joint."

A snort erupted from Kiki's mouth. Where did the kid come up with that stuff? Another laugh quickly followed. Eva giggled, covering her mouth with her fingers. Kiki doubled over, wrapping her arms around her stomach as gut-splitting laughter rolled out. The sound bordered on hysterical, but hopefully Eva didn't notice.

Kiki took a deep breath and wiped the tears from her cheeks. It didn't seem right to find joy in this circumstance, but she'd take it. Eva sighed out the last of her own giggles as she lay back against the filthy mattress.

"Do you think Uncle D is okay?" Eva's quiet question popped the joyful bubble and covered Kiki with miry disquiet.

"Of course, he's fine." Kiki smiled, though she no longer felt like it. "Don't forget, Eva-mine, Uncle D is one of the best super soldiers in the world. He probably has a plan all worked out to get us free." Kiki hoped using Derrick's nickname for Eva bolstered her spirits.

Loud cursing and shouts sounded outside. Kiki jerked from the wall and pulled herself to look out the window. A group of ragtag soldiers trailed into the clearing from the jungle. Their shoulders slumped in defeat, causing the giddiness of the moment before to bubble back to life in her chest. Some men kept darting uneasy glances at Edgar, who had stopped below a large tree, cussing and kicking the trunk in anger.

"What is it?" Eva pulled on Kiki's leg.

"It's the men." Kiki lowered herself and gathered Eva into a hug. "They didn't find Uncle D."

"We're gonna escape." Eva squeezed Kiki hard. "Do you think he'll break us free tonight?"

Kiki squatted so she'd be eye-level with Eva. "Honey, I don't know, but I bet he's doing everything he can to get us out. Do you know what that means?"

Eva shook her head.

"It means we need to be ready." Kiki kissed the top of Eva's head, then led her to the mattress. "We've had a busy day with little food for energy. Why don't we rest for a bit?"

"Uncle D said we should nap to keep our energy up," Eva said sagely.

Fifteen minutes later, Eva's soft snores floated next to Kiki. She rolled off the bed, trying to disturb the mattress as little as possible. Her mind raced with what ifs and made it impossible to fall asleep.

She didn't want to allow her mind to jet down the trail of dread her thoughts wanted her to venture on. She couldn't bring herself to play games anymore. With Eva sleeping, making the situation fun no longer held appeal.

She stood in the center of the small room with her eyes closed, focusing her thoughts and visualizing attacks. With slow, precise motions, she moved through counterattacks that Lena and Derrick had taught her. Taking care not to expend energy she might need later, she went through defensive and offensive maneuvers, repeating her friends' instructions in her head.

After running through all she could remember multiple times, she stretched onto the floor and worked through her morning yoga routine. The familiar moves calmed her even more and reinforced her determination. She might not be the amazing warrior Lena was, but she was stronger than most gave her credit for. That was a misconception she would take advantage of the first chance she got.

Footsteps stomped outside, and Kiki stood, forcing her heart to slow its rapid escalation. The lock rattled, and Edgar strode through the door. He shoved a tray of food at her. It tipped precariously, so she gripped the sides tightly. Could she use it as a weapon and escape with Eva through the open door?

"Your pathetic coward of a lover left you." Edgar sneered. "Ran fast like he couldn't get through the jungle quick enough." He let out an evil chuckle that raised the hair on Kiki's neck. "You need better taste in men, mamacita."

Kiki narrowed her eyes at the term. She'd never found the word endearing. She schooled her expression, hoping she achieved a look of innocence.

"So, you found him?" She couldn't help the disdain in her tone.

He glared. "He's halfway to Bogota by now."

"Sure he is." She smirked, then quickly smothered it. "I figured with your superior manhood, you'd have him in chains by now." She shrugged, her mind questioning her sanity. "Guess you overestimated yourself."

Edgar's face reddened as he lifted his fist. "Why you—"

"Edgar, Mathias wants a report." Marco stood in the doorway, his arms crossed and a bored look on his face.

Edgar growled and pointed a finger in her face. "I'm not done with you yet."

She held his glare with one of her own until he spun on his heel and stomped out the door.

Marco shook his head. "You'd better not poke that snake, señorita."

The door scraped along the concrete and clicked shut. The tray shook in her hands as all the tension rushed from her body. She set the food down before she dropped it and scrubbed her trembling hands over her face. What had she been thinking? Edgar might not be bright and colorful, but he was poisonous just the same.

## TWENTY-ONE

IT HAD TAKEN Derrick all day to circle back around to the complex. From his high vantage point on the cliff, he had scampered on to the large branches of the tall trees that still filled this area. He assumed this forest hadn't been stripped for lumber to hide the nefarious activities of the guerrillas, but he praised God for their existence as he worked his way from branch to branch like Tarzan until he made it back to the buildings.

He balanced against the trunk of a ceiba tree, hidden high in the canopy, and watched the people stomping back into the yard as dusk lengthened the shadows and lights blinked on in the huts and beach house. While the slow going had pinched his nerves, he had gotten great satisfaction in the frantic searching below him and the way Edgar had roared at the soldiers, cussing them out for their idiocy in losing Derrick's trail. Edgar had kicked the tree Derrick was in, his cursing rocketing to the treetops. Even hours later, that image threatened to push a snort of laughter from Derrick.

Now, though, the long hours of inching through the

branches and tedious waiting wore on him. His position in the tree gave him the perfect vantage point to watch the entire village. He'd almost come down when Edgar had taken a tray of food to Kiki and Eva, disappearing into the cell, only emerging when Marco approached the door. Two minutes, maybe less, but Derrick had nearly gone insane in those hundred and twenty-seconds.

He rubbed his hand over his prickly scalp, pushing the memory away ... again. No matter how hard he focused on his surveillance, those two minutes kept haunting him. Had Edgar hurt them? Marco had simply closed the door after Edgar left, so Derrick knew they weren't seriously injured.

Edgar made Derrick nervous. After the abduction, he'd thought Matias was the one that needed watched. Yet, Matias's cold, detached efficiency paled to the twisted, psychological comments and emotional outbursts exhibited by Edgar. Edgar proved a loose cannon, the one who would build in anger until he exploded his rage on those around him. That he'd focused so much attention on Derrick's little family troubled him. Derrick just hoped Edgar held his temper and sick desires until Derrick could get Kiki and Eva out of there.

Darkness settled over the repulsive village, and, except for a handful of men joking around a fire, the anthill of depravity slept. Could Derrick pick the lock and get Kiki and Eva free under the cover of night? He gritted his teeth. Marco sat in a chair leaned against the holding cell door. He might let Derrick in, but, with the light of the flame flickering brightly against the long building, the night guard would see any attempt to escape. The chance for failure was too high. Plus, whatever Marco's mission was, Derrick didn't want to compromise the agent's cover.

If Marco got Kiki and Eva on the yacht, Derrick could

get them free. His countless rescue missions in the army trained him for just that. First, before he inspected the yacht and secured a location for the following day, he had to check something.

Threading deeper into the forest to the tree he'd pinpointed earlier, Derrick climbed down the large trunk. The slow descent quelled his anxiety as he focused all his energy on lowering to the next branch. The darkness should have made him antsy, but he allowed the night sounds of the jungle and the cooler temperature to soothe him. He needed all the settling he could get before he did what needed done next.

He slinked along the path back to the complex, ready to disappear into the undergrowth at the slightest sound or motion. When the light from the campfire pushed the darkness of the jungle away, Derrick veered toward the large building where his company's mission had turned into a snafu.

Pushing the branch down, he refused to react at the sight of the door, and instead breathed a sigh of relief that it wasn't guarded. Did they only defend the building when prisoners were being held, or had the men been posted for the benefit of Derrick's unit? They had found out later that the mission had been compromised on purpose to hide the human trafficking happening beyond where the diplomat's family had been held.

Derrick ghosted to the back entrance of the building, preparing his heart for the dive into his nightmares. Easing the back door open, he crept into the building. Silence echoed loud in the open space of the barn turned holding pen, but the chaos of that day beat against his brain.

His eyes scanned the empty barn, half expecting the ghost of his friend Ethan to materialize in front of the opposite door. Not that Derrick believed in that kind of thing. He leaned against the rough wall behind him, closing his eyes against the pain of that fateful day.

Ethan's shocked face invaded Derrick's thoughts like it had for so long. He accepted that there had been nothing he could've done differently to save his friend. They were soldiers sent into the most dangerous situations. The risk of death had always been high.

Derrick had done what Ethan had asked, taking care of Lena, Ethan's fiancée. He'd made sure Lena found a place at the ranch after she retired from the military. The death of her fiancé had changed her from the woman always quick to lightheartedly rib others and passionate for the fight for freedom to someone cynical about life whose jabs were more sharp than funny. Derrick shook his head, pushing the heels of his hands against his eyes. That mission had changed them all.

"Come on, Goose," Derrick chided himself under his breath. "You have work to do."

He shook off the regret he thought he had conquered and rushed on silent feet across the barn. He slipped through the open doorway leading to the area his team hadn't known existed and pulled up short to the stench of unwashed bodies and excrement. There was no denying the space was used for holding people. Now, though, the room held nothing but the impression of those held and sold. How many people had waited here in despair? How many defeated souls had been dragged to the auction block behind the building Kiki and Eva slept in?

Slavery still had its talons gripped tight into the world. People would always take advantage of the weak. Didn't he see that every time he rescued a mistreated horse? Derrick had found his fight in the battle against evil, transforming the disparity of abuse into a path of healing for both horse and human.

He had accepted that he wasn't supposed to be a soldier anymore when he retired from the army. That didn't mean he couldn't cause a little chaos to this seedy operation. He smiled grimly. Once he got Kiki and Eva safe, he'd leave a mark of his own on the regime, hopefully helping Marco in his covert mission as Derrick escaped.

# TWENTY-TWO

"DO you think that prisoner will make it out of the jungle?" The question in Spanish from a guard posted on the dock made Derrick smirk as he swam beneath them toward the yacht.

His head bobbed low in the water, and he made his way toward the open garage on the side of the yacht. He'd spent some time creating diversions in the storage buildings scattered throughout the huts. It was a long shot that the makeshift explosives would be found while Derrick was here, but he had needed to do everything he could to increase his chances. Trusting Marco to get Kiki and Eva to the yacht had Derrick's head pounding with uncertainty.

"Nah, the jungle will take care of him." A gruff answer preceded the distinctive strike of a match lighting.

"I don't know. He got out of the handcuffs." Awe laced the first voice as he responded. "How did he do that?"

"However he did it left him covered in blood. That will attract a predator faster than Jose's beans cause the runs."

The two guffawed. Derrick could splash like a beached whale and they probably wouldn't hear above their conversation. Only four more feet and Derrick would be in the garage.

"Did you see Edgar's tantrum?" The conversation dropped to a hushed whisper.

What did the mercenaries think of Edgar's earlier display?

"He whines worse than my two-year-old niece."

They snickered.

"He's not right." The statement was low, like the guard worried Edgar would hear him.

"Completely loco. If you want to stay alive, keep out of Edgar's way."

Derrick shivered in the warm water. He couldn't wait to get his family far away from this place. He slipped into the garage, easing along the speedboat and pulling himself into the smaller rig. He had a better chance of escaping discovery if he didn't leave wet footsteps everywhere.

Lifting the cushion off the boat's couch, Derrick smiled around the small flashlight clamped in his teeth he'd scavenged. The stack of towels neatly folded would dry him off and erase his arrival. Quietly, he untied the make-shift bag he'd made of a tarp from one of the storage sheds and pulled his clothes from it. After drying any evidence of his arrival and shoving everything back under the cushion, he made his way through the yacht.

Anxious energy laced his muscles tightly as he searched the yacht. He listened at the first door he came to for any sign of movement. When he heard none, he turned the knob nice and slow and cracked the door. His heartbeat pounded in his ears, making it hard to hear.

*Calm down, man.*

He inched his light up from the floor into the rest of the room. Lifejackets, scuba gear, and motorized diving equipment lined the walls and shelves. He scanned the storage room for anything he could use, categorizing everything for the future. He didn't know how he'd get Kiki and Eva off the yacht once they were there, so he had to build several contingencies while he searched. He closed the door without a sound and moved down the hall.

*One down. Many more to go.*

With a yacht this size, there was no telling how many doors he'd be opening. He eased to the next door and repeated the process, only to be greeted by empty crew quarters. Where was the crew? Were the two men on the dock all that kept watch over the ship?

*Focus, D. Stay alert.*

He shut the door and continued his search. Exhaustion pulled at his brain and the slight rocking of the ship beckoned him to find a place and rest. Maybe he could rack out in one of the crew rooms. Derrick rolled his eyes at himself. There'd be time for sleep later.

His eyebrows rose as he peered into the next room. He shot into the space and shut the door. The computers lining the built-in desk, walkies, and keys hanging from the pegboard indicated he'd just found the security room. Striding to the desk, he pulled opened the drawers.

Four SAT phones sat stored in the bottom drawer. He closed his eyes and let out a quiet exhale. Maybe he could get some backup?

Checking the first one, he gritted his teeth when the screen flashed a red low-battery message. He checked the next one, only to have his heart drop a little more. *Come on.* The third screen blinked a dark blue before springing to life. Derrick leaned his forehead on the edge of the desk and squeezed his eyes closed. Had he ever felt such relief before? He shook off the emotion and dialed.

"Hello?" Zeke's tight voice coming through the phone clogged Derrick's throat with warring emotions.

He cleared the regret and relief away and pitched his voice low. "Zeke."

"D, man, thank God." The sound of snapping and moving bodies came over the speaker. "Where are you?"

"Colombia. That complex we rescued Hope Isaac from."

He heard mutterings from others. Zeke had him on speaker. Good, it'd save time.

"What happened?" Zeke's voice held an edge of emotion Derrick had never heard before.

Was it blame or despair? Whatever it was, Derrick had caused it. He'd do everything he could to fix it.

"They overpowered us." Derrick sighed and started sifting through the other drawers. "They were after Kiki and thought that Eva and I were her family. Something to do with Kiki's father."

"Are they okay?" Zeke's question squeezed Derrick's heart.

"At the moment." How could he tell one of his best friends his daughter was about to be trafficked? "There's an embedded operative here. CIA. He helped me escape. Promised me he'd keep an eye on Eva and Kiki and try to get them on the yacht docked here."

It now sounded like such a flimsy plan. Why hadn't he tried to get them free? They could be miles away by now. He shook his head. He had to trust, to let go of his need to control everything. At some point later that day, Marco would get Kiki and Eva on the yacht. Derrick had to do what he could to prepare.

"Something's happening later today. The yacht is

empty at the moment, so I'll be able to set up a means of escape."

"We won't be able to get down there until late morning or so." A loud huff sounded, blowing Zeke's frustration through the phone. "If you head out to sea before then ..."

*They might never be found.* Derrick finished the thought Zeke couldn't say. There had to be a way to track them.

"Can you track this SAT phone?"

"As long as you keep it on, we should be able to see your location." Rafe's sure tone eased Derrick's tight muscles.

He peeked at the phone's screen. "It has a full battery." He quickly opened the drawer with the phones and pulled out the last one. "I have another here that also has a full battery. I'll call you with it, so if this one dies, we have a backup."

"Good." Rafe's voice grew quiet as he talked, like he was rushing to his computers. "I'll contact the navy. Maybe there's a ship close."

Derrick prayed there was. He'd take a rescue from a frogman unit if it meant Eva and Kiki got home safe. He picked the lock on a tall cabinet, his mouth twitching when it swung open. The stash of weapons pumped hope through his blood.

"I've found the mother-load. I need to take advantage of the yacht being empty while I can." Derrick pulled weapons out of the cabinet and set them on the desk.

"We'll do what we can to help." Zeke's take-command tone was back. "We'll be in the air within the half hour."

"Zeke?" Guilt tightened Derrick's chest, making it hard to breathe.

"Yeah?" The change in sound said Zeke had taken the phone off speaker.

"I'm so sorry, man." Derrick cleared his throat. "I didn't assess the situation properly—had let my guard down."

"D, man, it could have happened to any of us." Zeke's soft answer made the band of guilt cinch taut.

"No, Zeke." Derrick had to get the confession out. "I wasn't on and let distractions pull my attention."

"Bright blue eyes and a soft smile will do that to a man." Zeke sighed. "I know you, man. Even distracted, you're the best there is. You can't change the past, D. Just do everything on your end to get you all home."

"Copy that." Derrick sniffed, blinking the stinging from his eyes. "I'll check in when I can."

"SASS, man," Zeke commanded before cutting the call.

The order to stay alert and stay safe settled over Derrick. Glancing at the stash of weapons, a plan formulated in his mind. His lips pressed into a grim smile. If he played it right, he could create chaos unlike any this group had ever seen before.

# TWENTY-THREE

A MONKEY SHRIEKED, followed by another, jerking Kiki awake. Sweat-soaked hair clung to her face and neck. The stench of an untold number of soiled bodies lifted from the mattress and filled her nose. She scowled as a lizard darted along the cinderblock wall. *Just another day in paradise.*

Would they get free before she had to lie on this filth another night? Had Derrick found a safe place? She rolled over and stood from the bed. She couldn't let the questions assault her again, not if she wanted to keep sane.

Footsteps approached, and the lock rattled. Someone was here already? She wiped the sweat from her neck and rolled her shoulders back. She couldn't give in to the urge to cower.

The door swung open, and Marco stepped in. *Thank God.* Relief loosened her muscles. She quickly tightened them back up. *Are you stupid or just dumb?* Marco was the enemy just as much as Edgar and Mathias. Just because he seemed nicer than the rest didn't mean he wouldn't hurt her or Eva.

"Come. The boss is waiting for you." Marco's gruff tone reinforced her inner chide.

She kneeled on the mattress and shook Eva's shoulder. "Eva, honey, it's time to wake up."

"Mommy?" Eva's sleepy question bit into Kiki's heart.

Would her sweet niece ever see her mom again?

"It's time to get up. We have to go for a walk." Kiki motioned with her head at Marco when Eva's eyes finally blinked open.

Eva's eyes widened, then she turned her face into her hands. Her tiny shoulders shook as quiet sobs filled the dreary space. Kiki's vision blurred as she reached for Eva.

"I want *my* daddy." Eva's emphasis on just what dad she wanted wasn't lost on Kiki.

At least the smart darling was brave enough not to blow their secret. Kiki would have to be fearless, push the trepidation and pain aside so she could keep Eva safe. She didn't know what this so-called boss wanted, but Kiki was prepared to sacrifice anything for Eva's protection.

"We have to go." Marco's statement held annoyance and a hint of something else. Fear? Maybe.

Kiki pulled Eva into her arms, determined not to let whatever she detected in Marco's tone affect her. Eva wrapped her arms and legs around Kiki and buried her tear-soaked face into Kiki's neck. When they got out of this and she left the ranch, she had a few things she wanted to say to her father before she disappeared forever. Maybe she'd find some mission or nunnery or something where she could not only hide but do the world some good. Not that anything she did would balance the evil her family was steeped in.

Marco led them from the cell, the bright sun blinding Kiki as it rose above the trees. Her mind whirled with possibilities as she followed Marco toward the beach house.

Could she buy their freedom? While she didn't have nearly as much as her father had, she had a good nest egg accumulated after years of trading. Surely it was enough for two lives. If not, sixty-million plus definitely could ensure for one little life to be spared, couldn't it? Kiki would squeeze her accounts dry if it meant Eva went free.

"You need to get her to stop crying." Marco glared back at Kiki. "The boss hates crying."

"If he doesn't like crying, maybe he should stop stealing children and women," Kiki shot back before she smoothed her hand over Eva's hair. "Honey, you need to be brave."

"But I'm scared," Eva whimpered against Kiki's neck.

"I know, honey. I'm scared too." Kiki choked down her own wail. "We can't let these jerks win, Eva-mine. We can't let them see our weakness."

"Be strong and courageous, just like Daddy told me." Eva sniffed, wiping her arm under her nose.

"Do not be dismayed." Kiki gave Eva a squeeze.

Eva wiped her face on Kiki's shirt, causing Kiki to both cringe and chuckle. Eva wiggled free, slid her small hand in Kiki's, and walked with her chin high. Samantha would be so proud of Eva right now. Her mother's strength shone through her face and filled Kiki with pride.

*Be strong. Be courageous.* If Kiki kept the chant up, maybe she could succeed at both.

A distant thumping caught Kiki's attention as they approached the grand house. She shaded her eyes from the sun with her hand and peered out over the ocean. The silhouette of a helicopter flying in gave her a jolt of anticipation. Was it a rescue party? Kiki shook her head and focused on the path before her. It wasn't hiding its advance on the area, so it had to be someone within the organization.

Kiki climbed the stairs to the house's deck, her rapid

pulse making her lightheaded. What would the boss be like? Would he attack them right away? Would he have buyers lined up and waiting? She stumbled over the images barraging her mind and gripped the handrail.

*Be strong. Be courageous.*

The shaded deck had luxurious furniture scattered throughout. Sheer curtains creating areas of semi-privacy around clumps of chairs floated in the morning breeze. A woman dressed in a gauzy sundress with a plunging neckline reclined in a lounge chair. A large-brimmed hat covered her face. Was she a captive as well? She lifted her head to watch their approach, a blank expression on her face.

"Aunt Jackie?" Kiki stopped short, and confusion flooded her brain, making it race with broken thoughts.

"Kiki. How nice to see you again." Her father's sister lifted the hat from her head and gently laid it on the side table laden with fresh coffee and fruit.

"What? I don't—" Kiki shook her head to jiggle her thoughts in order.

"Have you enjoyed our accommodations?" The sinister gleam in Aunt Jackie's eyes countered the sweet smile on her face.

"You knew we were here?" Pain bit into Kiki's palm as she dug her fingernails into her hand.

"Of course I knew, you ninny." Jackie *tsked* and shook her head like she was disappointed. "I had such high hopes for you. I always wanted you to take over in my stead, tried to groom you for it, but you were too much a goody two shoes."

Memories of Aunt Jackie giving Kiki attention growing up assaulted her mind. She'd loved the extra attention. Had savored the visits, spending time with the aunt that doted on her like neither of her parents had. Kiki rubbed her hand over her chest as vulnerability left her exposed.

"I had to abandon the venture for a lost cause and had hoped your brother would be more suited." Jackie examined her nails. "Shame he didn't like following orders. Seems to be a family habit. His death was a hard command to issue."

All the blood rushed from Kiki's head, and she forced herself not to collapse. She had never observed such false emotion as what flitted across Jackie's face. Her gaze landed on Eva and a predatory grin pushed the evil woman's cheeks up. Kiki pulled Eva closer. How could Kiki have been so wrong about all her family? The wicked delight splashed across her aunt's face tightened the cinch that the family lies had tied around Kiki's neck. This time it might just strangle her.

## TWENTY-FOUR

DERRICK PEERED out the small window from the room used as storage on the yacht. He had done all he could the night before to scope out the layout and set diversions. When a small crew led by a stoic Mattias and a shouting Edgar filtered onto the boat in the early morning hours, Derrick had abandoned his reconnaissance to lie low. He had several escape plans mapped out in his head, if only things would fall into place.

He had holed up in a storage room for movies, books, and other things of nefarious nature he'd rather not think about. Its location, close to the engine room and only a floor below where prisoners supposedly were kept, would work into his plan. The tactical gear he'd stolen from the security room hung heavy on his body with enough artillery to start a small war. None of it brought any comfort.

"Just trust, man." He adjusted his grip on the rifle as the thumping of a helicopter landing on the yacht drowned out all other sounds.

When he'd spied Kiki and Eva being led to the beach house, he'd almost abandoned his plans and stormed from his hiding spot. Kiki's confused and desperate expressions had had his teeth gritting with his inability to help her. His only comfort was that Marco stood at Kiki's side.

Derrick peered through the rifle's scope again, observing the woman gesturing toward Eva. When he'd first noticed her sitting on the lounge chair without a care in the world, he'd guessed she was the boss's wife or girlfriend. Yet the way Kiki had reacted said the woman was much more than what he'd expected. Their voices had been too low to hear, especially with the helicopter now gearing down. The woman stalked from Kiki and Eva and peered toward the yacht.

Adjusting his gaze to see the dock, Derrick flinched at the sight of Matias leading Kevin and Cynthia Payne with Edgar following. What were Kiki's parents doing at this demonic, tropical getaway? He darted his eyes to Kiki. She pushed Eva behind her and lifted her head high.

"That's my girl." Derrick encouraged her, though she couldn't hear.

"Brother, so glad you could join us," the woman called, her cheery greeting ringing false.

Brother? This woman was Kiki's aunt? Why in the world would her aunt be involved with abducting Kiki?

"Jackie, this is totally unnecessary." Kevin motioned to Kiki and back toward the helicopter. "You know the feds are breathing down my neck. This little stunt of yours might have just nailed my coffin closed."

A salty breeze blew in through the small opening, carrying the conversation over the water to Derrick. It did nothing to cool his sweaty skin. The look on Jackie's face froze him to the core, though.

"Kevin, when you don't return my calls, other measures

must be taken." Jackie paced in front of Kevin as he stopped on the porch.

Cynthia leaned against the glass railing of the deck, her nose crinkling as she scanned the huts lining the jungle's edge. She held the same bored look she'd had when she and Kevin had video-conferenced with Samantha about getting custody of Eva. Did the woman not take anything seriously?

"In case you've forgotten, I have a lot on my plate, Jackie." Kevin pushed his fingers through his hair.

"I'm well aware of the mess you've gotten yourself into, Brother." Even at a distance, her voice dripped with venom. "You should've left the brat alone and not drawn attention to yourself."

She paced up to Mattias and ran her hand down his chest before turning back to her brother and crossing her arms. Whatever she said didn't carry to Derrick, but Kevin didn't like it. His ears turned red and hands clenched into fists at his side.

"What does the company expect me to do, Jackie?" Kevin's frustrated yell held a tinge of fear to it.

Was this company he spoke of the same organization that had botched Derrick's last mission at this complex? The same group that had tried to steal June's invention? Had the Paynes been involved all this time and Stryker Security Force hadn't known? Marco's presence made more sense now. Was he part of General Paxton's covert team?

"The feds are crawling all over my place." Kevin's voice had turned whiny and pulled Derrick's attention back to the conversation. "They've posted men at all my oil platforms and shut down all my operations. We won't be able to hold new acquisitions at the platforms anymore. It'll be years before I'm out from under this."

"Then I guess the company no longer has a use for you."

In one smooth motion, Jackie pulled Mattias's handgun from his holster and put two bullets into her brother.

Shrieking, Cynthia rushed up to Kevin's body, unaware of the gun now turned on her. Marco stepped forward and motioned to the yacht. Derrick let a whoosh of air slowly from his mouth and took aim through the scope, putting Jackie's heart in the crosshairs. He'd give Marco five seconds to deescalate the situation before Derrick opened fire. Why hadn't he found a better location? He should've never stayed trapped on the boat.

Kiki positioned herself behind Marco with Eva pressed to her back. Derrick pushed the way Eva'd buried her face into Kiki's shirt from his thoughts. He ignored Kiki's wide eyes and gaped mouth. If he didn't focus, he'd never get his loved ones to safety.

An explosion blasted in the village, jerking everyone's attention toward the jungle. Derrick smiled in satisfaction and sent a quick thanks to heaven. His makeshift bomb couldn't have gone off at a better time.

"Marco, take care of that infuriating man once and for all," Jackie ordered Marco, pointing toward the huts. She motioned to Kiki, Eva, and a still-sobbing Cynthia. "Get them on the yacht. We're leaving."

Derrick snapped the rifle down and sagged in relief. Though he'd rather have Marco as backup for the next part of the rescue plan, Derrick could at least breathe now that Kiki and Eva were heading his way. He stared at Kiki as the group rushed down the dock, willing her to not lose hope. Praying he didn't make another fatal mistake.

# TWENTY-FIVE

KIKI CLUNG TO EVA, cataloging everything as Edgar led them through the yacht. She had to find a way off the ship, had to remember every detail she could. Derrick wouldn't be rescuing them, not with how far off the blast had been.

Biting the inside of her cheek to keep from bawling like her mother, she pushed the crushing terror and grief down. She couldn't get Eva to safety if she fell apart now. Edgar led them down a hall past a room with two men wearing guns slung across their chest.

"¿Que pasa?" One guard asked Edgar, pointing toward shore. "What's happening out there?"

"Her man is attempting a rescue mission." Edgar leered at Kiki and winked. "Too bad we'll be far out to sea before he can get through the men."

The two guards laughed with Edgar as he grabbed Kiki's elbow and pulled her down the hall. Her mother's fingers twisted in the back of Kiki's shirt. Her grip hadn't eased since Kiki had yanked her mother off her father's body. Kiki shuddered as the image of her father's shocked face assaulted her.

*Stop, Kiki. Focus.*

Right. Two guards stood at the end of the hallway. Just like the bottom level. She had seen no other men, not that that meant they weren't there. Still, if she could get them free and get to the speedboat parked in the garage on the back end, they'd escape.

Halfway down the hall, Edgar opened a door to a bedroom. "Your room. Better than the last one, eh?"

Kiki pushed her mom into the room, where she collapsed onto the floor in a wailing heap. Kiki stepped to follow, only to have Edgar pull her back to him. He rubbed his thumb up and down the inside of her arm. The touch raced along her skin like a hundred cockroaches.

"I'll be seeing you later, mamacita." His hot whisper against her neck had angry heat rising up her chest.

She yanked her arm away and stepped backward into the room. Narrowing her eyes at the satisfaction that lifted the side of his mouth in a smirk, the fury spread from her chest to her limbs. She held his repulsive stare with an icy one of her own.

"I'm looking forward to it." Her voice held a steely calm she'd never heard before.

Hooking the door with her foot, she slammed it in his confused face. She peeled Eva off of her and set the trembling child on the bed, turning to the door just in case he came back in. She wanted to be ready to attack.

Could she get off the yacht before it got far from the shore and find Derrick?

The sound of a lock clicking on the door released all the tension from her body, and she collapsed to the bed. Eva crawled into Kiki's lap, her small frame trembling in Kiki's arms. The soft hum of the ship's motor and the lurch as it left the dock settled in Kiki's gut.

They wouldn't be meeting up with Derrick ... couldn't be counting on him to come to the rescue. Eva's escape landed solidly in Kiki's ill-equipped hands. She closed her eyes and pulled Eva tighter.

*"You have to toughen up."* Lena's words in the training room rolled through Kiki's head. *"Can't neutralize a larger enemy if you aren't willing to use all your skills."*

The defenseless, pampered socialite from the fall didn't exist anymore, not with all the drilling Kiki had gone through over the months. She may not be as prepared for danger as Lena and Derrick and the others, but she couldn't be called softie either. Couldn't she shoot the target with regular accuracy at the range? Hadn't she taken down Derrick when he'd surprised her? What could she do when she planned her attack?

Kiki's eyes snapped open and scanned the room. She had more than enough to work with. As plans and preparations raced through her brain like stocks on her computer screens, her muscles tightened with the need to act. Her lips lifted in a hard smile. Edgar couldn't visit fast enough.

# TWENTY-SIX

"ZEKE, WE'RE ON THE MOVE." Derrick's whisper floated just above inaudible.

He couldn't risk anyone hearing, but also needed to update the team and see if he'd have reinforcements. The engine's whining acceleration and muffled water crashing against the hull built an anxious fluttering in his core. Had he made the right decision in not breaking Kiki and Eva out the night before? Now they all were trapped in this floating prison.

"We have your signal locked, but we won't be able to get you help for at least an hour, man, maybe more." Zeke's frustration built the fluttering to full-on churning.

Derrick puffed his cheeks and blew out his disappointment. He'd just have to embrace the suck. It hadn't been the first time and wouldn't be the last.

"I have an exit plan." Kind of.

"The brass wants you to stay on the yacht as long as possible so they can track where they take you." Zeke's voice vibrated with contained anger.

"Good thing I'm not enlisted anymore." Derrick had

loved the army, but this request settled like sawdust in his mouth. "I'm getting Eva and Kiki out of here. I won't risk it."

Banter sounded in the hall out the door, and Derrick slipped behind the door. He'd picked the supply room because of the toys used while at anchor. He wasn't quite ready for the boat's occupants to know he wasn't back at the village yet.

"Thanks, D." Zeke's words twisted in Derrick's heart. It was his fault Zeke's daughter was here. "When you get free, head southwest. There's a carrier about a hundred klicks from you. Can't get any closer than that without causing problems with the locals. We're also heading toward you on a yacht."

"Roger," Derrick muttered before ending the call.

The voices drew closer, excitement about being able to catch some soccer game since they were on the yacht bouncing between them. Maybe Derrick would catch a break, and the game would distract the crew. How long did he have before someone from the village reported back to Kiki's aunt that Derrick wasn't there? Would Marco be able to send the men on a wild goose chase and give Derrick time?

The men passed, and Derrick counted to a hundred. Should he hold and let them settle into the ride, or should he put his plan into action now? An unfamiliar edge of impatience prodded him to move. He'd gotten control of his jitters his first year in the special ops team. Having them return now left him unsettled.

Derrick almost missed the footsteps as they approached the door. When they stopped on the other side, Derrick stared at the handle, willing himself to focus and his heart rate to slow down. The handle turned and the clatter of a gun knocking against the door preceded a man entering the storage room. He quickly scanned the hall like he didn't want anyone to see him entering and closed the door.

His eyes widened when they landed on Derrick. Derrick struck, thrusting his elbow into the man's throat and gripping the AR-15 slung across his body so it didn't clang. As the crew member gasped for breath, Derrick slid behind the man. He had to be silenced before Derrick's entire mission blew apart before it even started. He wrapped his arm across his opponent's neck and within seconds the man went limp.

After setting him on the ground, Derrick stepped to the door and listened. Satisfied no one had heard, he hid and secured the man so he couldn't alert anyone. Looked like Derrick's hiding place wasn't such a great one.

He double checked his gear was still intact and slung the AR over his shoulder. He hadn't taken much from the security room, not wanting to alert anyone to his presence. The familiar weight of the bigger gun against his chest calmed him.

He couldn't hold off any longer. If he continued to wait, someone else might stumble upon him. As it was, his plan would take time to set in motion. With a quick prayer for protection, he eased the door open, scanned the hall, and darted toward the engine room.

# TWENTY-SEVEN

KIKI SURVEYED the room for anything she could use as a weapon. The sparse room held little hope of help. The stripped mattress pushed against the outer wall didn't even have a pillow. At least it wasn't filthy like the one in the cinderblock room. Kiki cringed. As far as she could tell.

"How could she do this?" Her mom let out a hysterical wail. "Turning on her own flesh and blood."

Kiki clamped her lips shut and stepped into the bathroom. What did her mom expect? Working with an organization as sick as the one her family seemed steeped in could only lead to terrible places. Kiki swallowed down her own grief, refusing to let it distract her from escaping.

The bathroom held the same as the bedroom ... nothing but a half-used roll of toilet paper and a sliver of soap. She yanked on the towel rack. The bar could prove useful, but it didn't budge.

She sighed as she stepped back into the bedroom, her gaze landing on Eva on the bed. Her black curls tumbled wildly around her dark face streaked with tears. Her eyes widened at Kiki and bounced to Kiki's mom, Eva's grandma, like she would bite. Kiki didn't blame Eva. The family had brought nothing but heartache to Eva's door.

"Eva, honey, it's going to be all right." Kiki sat on the bed and pulled Eva onto her lap. "I'm going to get us out of here."

"But, but that lady shot that man." Eva buried her face in Kiki's neck. "What if they shoot us too?"

Kiki closed her eyes, wishing she could take away the last days from Eva's memory. Wishing she could've stopped her parents months before when they had claimed Eva as their own. Then Eva would have been safe.

Of course, if her parents hadn't pushed Eva's mom into a corner, she never would have left Texas. She and Zeke never would've married, and Eva wouldn't have the amazing family of "uncles" that doted on her. Kiki never would've found out what a true family looked like. She wouldn't let Eva lose that.

"I'm getting us out of here, Eva-mine." Kiki pushed Eva's shoulders back so she could look her in the eyes. "I promise, I'm getting you home."

Eva's nod was slow coming, but when it did, Kiki smiled.

"I'm going to need your help." Kiki rubbed her thumb over Eva's cheek. "We are going to have to be brave."

"I can be brave." Eva swiped the back of her hand under her nose.

"You're the bravest person I know, Eva."

Kiki flinched when her mother let out another wail. If she didn't pull it together, Kiki wouldn't be able to escape, at least not with her mom in tow. Could Kiki leave her behind? If it was between that and getting Eva free, Kiki wouldn't have a choice.

"Mom." Kiki set Eva on the mattress and stood.

"How could she? After all that we've done for her?" Her mom's voice filled with hate. "She'd be nothing without everything Kevin did for her."

Well, there went the idea that her mother wasn't involved. Kiki's stomach flipped on itself. How had she been such a naive fool? She was just as selfish as the rest of them, so focused on the material that she hadn't cared where it came from. Kiki's skin crawled, and she felt dirty, like she'd never be clean again.

"Mom." She stepped closer, needing to come up with a plan to get Eva far away from their taint before it ruined her too.

Her mother buried her head into her hands. Kiki's disgust with herself burned away as fiery anger filled her chest. Either her mom helped, or Kiki left her behind and let whatever consequence awaited happen. Kiki closed the distance between them and jabbed her mother's shoulder.

"Mom, stop." Kiki crossed her arms over her chest so she didn't do something uncalled for, like slap her mother across the face.

Kiki smirked. That might hold merit. She let her arms drop. She'd been hanging around Lena too much.

Her mom glared up at Kiki. "This is all your fault."

"No, mom." Kiki took a step back to keep control of the emotions threatening to strike out. "I'm not letting you lay this on me."

"If you would've just done what we said, the feds wouldn't be breathing down our necks, and this never would've happened." Her mother stood, the icy stare piercing Kiki's heart and making her shudder.

Kiki gazed at her mom, her eyes stinging. When had decency abandoned her mother? She'd always been distant, preferring to let the nanny raise her children, but there had been times of devotion, hadn't there? Fundraisers and concerts sprang to mind, all followed by the sense of calculation Kiki had gotten at those events. Like her family's involvement was less about the charity and more about the connections gained.

"Your father is dead because of you," her mother spat, pushing her normally perfect hair out of her face.

Kiki balled her hands and stepped toward her mother. The easily manipulated girl no longer existed. Either her mother would get on board, or Kiki would take her down too. She jabbed Cynthia in the chest.

"I am not taking the blame for your sins, Mother." The name dripped with disgust from her mouth. "I'm getting us out of here, but I won't hesitate to leave you behind."

"You wouldn't."

"In a heartbeat." Kiki stepped back. "Getting Eva safe is all that matters."

"How do you expect to overtake a boat full of mercenaries?" Cynthia's arms motioned wide.

"You forget where I've been living."

Kiki took stock of Cynthia's outfit. The three-inch spike heels, thick gold strands adorning her neck, and gaudy signature scarf might come in handy.

"Take off your shoes and necklaces." Kiki motioned to the articles. "You won't be able to escape with those shoes, and I could use them as weapons."

"And what are you going to do with the jewelry, pay them off?" Cynthia's condescending tone grated.

"No. But they might be helpful in strangling them."

Kiki ignored the sputtering and pulled the razor blade from its hiding place in her shoe. She had to work quick. Edgar or someone else could come at any minute. She sliced the mattress, quickly stripping the wire from the edge. As she pulled the wire free, the door swung open.

"Were you threatening—" Edgar's question cut short as his gaze took in the room, his thick black eyebrows winging upward in shock.

Without hesitation, Kiki stepped into Edgar's space, slapping his reaching hand aside with one fist, and ramming the other into his chin just like Lena had taught her. Edgar's eyes rolled back into his head and he flopped to the floor.

"Quick! Grab the door before it closes," Kiki hissed to Cynthia.

With a squeak, she grabbed the door a second before it shut. Kiki flipped Edgar onto his stomach and pulled his hands behind his back. Motioning to Eva to toss her the mattress wire, she wrapped it tight around his wrists then his ankles like she had seen in the westerns Derrick forced her to watch. The wire dug into the sleaze's skin, but she didn't care.

"Give me your scarf." She pointed to the brightly colored accessory and wrapped Edgar's mouth with it so he couldn't scream for help when he came to.

She unholstered his gun, checked that there was a bullet in the chamber, then pocketed the extra magazine from Edgar's belt. She'd rather not have to use the weapon, but she would if she had to. After shoving the high heels into her back pockets, she motioned for Eva to join her and stepped toward her shocked mom.

"Who are you?" Cynthia whispered, her tone full of awe.

"I'm finally who I was meant to be." Kiki cocked the gun. "You follow real close and keep a hold of Eva. If you don't keep up or if you freak out, I will not hesitate to take her myself and leave you. Understand?"

Cynthia nodded, her gaze darting to Eva. Could Kiki trust her? Probably not, but she needed her hands free to work the weapon. She gave Eva a quick hug, then stepped to the door.

She could hear a holler of a score followed by cheering and groaning from farther down the hall. A man leaned against a doorframe, watching whatever game was playing in the room. Could they get down the corridor to the stairs without him noticing? She motioned to her mother to follow. With a deep breath, she stepped from the room.

# TWENTY-EIGHT

DERRICK SLIPPED from the engine room. The distractions he'd set up early ticked down, leaving him little time to locate Kiki before things started hopping. His scouting had told him if he could get to the second floor without being detected, he'd only have a handful of barren rooms to check. He cleared the hall and stalked down it just as the door to the security room snapped open.

Derrick pushed the man back into the room, shoving him into the desk with a crash. Kicking a second man scrabbling from the chair in the head, Derrick slammed the first man's head into the desk. Heaving hard, Derrick whipped the zip ties he'd found from his pocket and secured the men.

A walkie lying on the floor sounded with static before Mattias's voice spoke. "José, the boss wants you on the top deck."

Derrick's window of opportunity had just shortened. He checked the hall and dashed out.

*Hustle. Second floor. Get the girls. Get out.*

He peeked into the stairwell, only to freeze. Kiki rushed down the stairs, followed by her mother carrying Eva. He stepped on the stairs in a daze. How had they gotten free? Cynthia squeaked, causing Kiki to flinch and raise a gun. Where had she gotten a gun? A slight moan escaped her before she ran down the remaining stairs and threw herself into his arms. Her kiss was quick but seared him to his soul.

"How'd you get here?" She pulled back, her forehead crinkling in confusion.

"I've been here all along."

"But the village, the explosion?"

"Just a diversion."

She nodded, her face determined though her body trembled. "What's the plan?"

Man, how he loved her.

"We take the helo. There's a navy vessel south of here waiting for us. I set up more surprises that should go off any minute." He glanced at his watch and cringed.

Would they make it to the helo in time? That hadn't been his original plan, but escaping in the helicopter would get them farther faster than the speedboat. She looked back at her mother, then turned to him.

"I'll bring up the rear." She motioned for him to lead up the stairs.

He hated that idea, but couldn't help it. Tweaking Eva's nose as he passed, he led them the way they had come. He could hear jovial shouting at the far end of the hall. He rounded the corner to sprint to the next floor as shots slammed into the wall behind him, followed by two quick return shots.

*No. Kiki.* Cynthia clung to Eva as she turned the corner and climbed the stairs. Kiki jumped into the stairwell as chaos exploded from the other end of the hall.

"Go!" she yelled, jerking him out of his panic.

He cleared the next level, taking out two men rushing

toward them. Why hadn't his first diversion gone off? One more floor to get to the landing pad. Three, maybe four guns fired behind him with Kiki keeping constant return fire.

"I'm out," Kiki hollered as they reached the deck.

"Kiki." He tossed her the AR and darted for the helicopter.

Bullets sprayed behind him, followed by another set of following feet. When he got to the helicopter, he grabbed Eva from Cynthia, pointed to the seat, and quickly went to work unfastening the tie-down straps from the skids. He vaulted into the pilot's seat, flipping switches to fire the bird up. Kiki climbed into the door, sitting in the opening, on guard.

"Stop!" Jackie emerged from the stairs, her gun pointed at the helicopter and fury etched on her face. "Get out of the helicopter now."

The rotor revved up, and the blades started their slow spin. *Come on. Faster.* Derrick opened the throttle completely.

"We're leaving," Kiki yelled over the engine. "Don't make me shoot you."

Derrick's heart clenched at the anguish in Kiki's voice. He glanced over his shoulder. Could he help her, keep her from doing something that would haunt her forever?

"You don't have the nerve." Her aunt stepped closer, adjusting her grip on her gun.

"You're wrong."

An explosion filled the air and rocked the yacht in a violent heave. He couldn't have timed the diversion better if he'd tried. Jackie tumbled to the deck, her gun skittering across the wood. Derrick lifted on the collective and pressed the left pedal.

"Hang on!" There was no way to smooth out this take off.

Bullets pinged off the metal of the bird as it lifted off. Derrick gripped the cyclic and propelled the helo forward. Another explosion ripped through the air as they cleared the yacht's railing, flames shooting straight into the sky.

Kiki slammed the door closed and was climbing into the co-pilot seat when the entire yacht burst into a ball of fire. What in the world? That wasn't supposed to happen. Cynthia screamed in back as Kiki crashed into him. She scrambled off as sensors beeped and yelled in his ears. Regaining control, he circled wide to get them pointed south. He scanned the debris of the yacht for survivors, but found nothing. Could their nightmare finally be over?

# TWENTY-NINE

KIKI GAPED out the window at the floating remains of the yacht. No one could survive that, could they? She should feel more remorse for Jackie's death, but Kiki was too light-headed with relief to process the complications of her sordid family tree.

"Diversion?" She turned to Derrick, who piloted the helicopter farther away from land.

His cheek flexed, and he shook his head. "I just set the two bombs." He gazed at her, regret in his eyes. "They were just supposed to disable the vessel enough to get us free and allow the navy to make arrests. They must've been storing something I missed during recon last night."

Kiki checked on Eva. Her wide eyes bounced between Derrick and Kiki. With her knees drawn up to her chest, she appeared so small. Was she truly safe now?

"We needed your aunt for information." The desperation in his voice slammed Kiki's heart like an anvil.

"But Eva is safe, right?" She dropped her voice, hoping Eva wouldn't hear.

Derrick peered at her, tension stretching between them so thick she couldn't breathe. He shrugged. *No.* She flopped back into the seat. This had to be over. There had to be a way to make Eva safe from the evil her family joined in.

"Well, I can tell you all about Jackie." Cynthia huffed a disdainful laugh, turning Kiki in her seat to see her mom's face. "Your aunt thought she was so smart. Thought I was just some dumb arm candy her brother kept for looks. I was the one who told your father what to do. He didn't have any real vision until I came along. Want to know why the boat blew up?" Her lip lifted in an unattractive sneer. "There were black market weapons in a secret storage compartment under the engine. I know where they were taking us. I know who her boss was. I know everything."

She pushed her shoulders back and smoothed her hair. Her expression mirrored Jackie's when she'd so flippantly killed Kiki's father that a shiver raced across Kiki's skin. She didn't know this person sitting behind her. Probably never had. Maybe Cynthia Payne held the answer to Eva's freedom.

Derrick leaned forward and tapped the dash. His forehead crinkled in concern. What could go wrong now? They were rendezvousing with the navy. They'd escaped, hadn't they?

"We have a little problem." Derrick's calm voice did nothing to ease the nervous energy rushing through Kiki's body.

"No. No more problems." She shook her head, the roar of her heartbeat battling the thumping of the helicopter blades. "I've had my fill of problems."

"I know, honey. Me too." Derrick's term of endearment and the lift of the side of his mouth soothed her zinging nerves. "But, we're losing fuel ... fast."

"What?" She jerked her gaze out the window to look at the tail of the helicopter, like she'd be able to see a stream of fuel gushing to the sea.

"Bullet must've hit the tank." Derrick flipped switches and spoke nonsense into his headset.

"Aunt Kiki?" Eva's trembling voice pulled Kiki's attention from Derrick. "Are we going to crash?"

She shook her head, her mouth opening to ease the fear on Eva's face, but nothing came out. What could Kiki say? What would happen if they ran out of fuel? Could they somehow jump before the death trap went down? Did the seats work as a flotation device like they did in airplanes? Kiki couldn't answer Eva—couldn't give her false hope.

"Eva-mine, we're not crashing," Derrick hollered. "Your dad is close. Rented some fancy yacht to save us in. If we can't make it to him, we'll just land this hunk of metal on the sea and wait for him to come pick us up."

"Daddy's here?" Eva uncurled and searched out the window.

"Yep, not too far away." Derrick glanced at the gauges before snapping his eyes back out the windshield. Was Zeke really close or was Derrick just saying that to ease Eva's fears?

"You can land on the water?" Kiki leaned over to peer at the red blinking light. The line hovered on the bottom of the gauge.

"I'll ditch it, if I have to." He pushed her hair behind her ear, then gripped the stick again. "Pray that I don't."

Kiki's body shook as she sat back in her seat. Her eyes frantically scanned the sea, searching for whatever Zeke was waiting on. Her mind raced with gruesome scenarios and desperate prayers. Each minute stretched impossibly long as more alarms blared loudly in the cockpit. Something glittered on the horizon, and her hand jerked toward it.

"There." The word squeezed past the fear lodged in her throat as a croak.

The helicopter shuddered as it flew toward the yacht in the distance. Sweat slid down Derrick's cheek, his teeth gritting. Would they crash and die so close? *No, please God, help.*

As they grew closer, she made out Zeke with his arm around Sam, and Rafe, Sosimo, and Jake on the deck watching them approach. Rafe waved his arm high, then clapped Jake on the back. Kiki relaxed her grip on the dash. They were going to make it.

"Hang on." Derrick's muscles bunched as the helicopter finally hovered over the yacht.

The engine cut, and Kiki squeezed the seatbelt in her hands. The only sound that reached her ears was the turning of the blades and her harsh breaths. Would they crash into the yacht and kill everyone? She wanted to squeeze her eyes closed but couldn't.

With smooth movements of his arms and legs, Derrick touched the helicopter down with a soft jolt. Eva's screams pierced the cockpit as the helicopter skid across the deck, hooked into the railing, and teetered over the edge of the yacht.

Rafe latched on to the skid beside her, the veins popping from his neck as he strained to hold the helicopter. Jake grabbed the skid next to Rafe. They couldn't possibly hold an entire helicopter. The door slid open with a swoosh, and Kiki turned to see Zeke unbuckle her mom and lift her from her seat.

"Daddy!" Eva's frightened sob ratcheted Kiki's own fear up another notch.

"It's going to be okay, honey," Zeke choked out, rushing tears back into Kiki's eyes.

Kiki turned forward and fumbled with her seatbelt as Derrick climbed into the back to help Eva. The helicopter lurched, tipping more toward the ocean and sending a chill across her sweaty skin. They were going to plummet into the ocean after all.

Her hands shook so violently she couldn't get the buckle unlatched. The screech as the skids scraped on the railing raced down her back like fingernails on a blackboard. She yanked on the belt as the guys yelled, and Sosimo pulled Rafe and Jake away from the helicopter.

"Hold on!" Derrick hollered above the crash of the railing collapsing.

Her eyes widened and her stomach floated into her throat as they fell toward the cerulean blue beneath them. Why hadn't Derrick jumped out? They were about to crash, and he wasn't buckled in.

The windshield splashed into the water, jerking her forward. The slam of her body against the harness knocked the air out of her. Her scream cut short as water rushed around her and filled her mouth. She spat out the water and tipped her face up, gasping in one large breath before the water came up over her head.

The sudden envelopment of water floated her in her seat. Would she drown when they'd been so close to safety? She thrashed at the buckle, but it still wouldn't budge.

*Oh, God, please.*

She didn't want to die.

Derrick's hand settled over hers, stilling their frantic fumbling. Her scream filled her head and threatened to push out, but she kept her mouth shut. He'd get her out. He wouldn't let her drown.

He worked the buckle. When it didn't budge, he jerked it hard. Dark spots swam before her eyes. At least she wouldn't die alone.

Derrick pulled a knife from somewhere and hacked at the straps. Her ears popped, and the cockpit darkened. They were sinking too far. He had to go before he drowned down here with her.

She needed to breathe, to open her mouth and let air in. She swallowed the urge but didn't think she could hold out much longer. Her lungs burned like hot lava. She should just give in.

One less Payne populating the world.

The sudden release of the strap almost caused her to gulp. Strong hands pulled her from the seat, then she was clamped against Derrick's body and moving fast. She wanted to help, wanted to hold on or kick, but all her muscles were limp.

Hands grabbed her from behind. Were they angels taking her to heaven? No. She thrashed and clung tight to Derrick's neck. She wasn't ready to die, wasn't ready to leave him.

They broke the surface, the sudden bright sun blinding her. She sucked in blessed air, only to violently cough so hard she was sure her ribs would crack. She didn't realize she was sobbing until Derrick pushed the hair out of her face and shushed her.

"It's okay." He pulled her close, his legs scissoring below hers. "We're safe now."

Kiki's chin trembled as she glanced around and noticed the guys had dived in after them. Eva hollered for Kiki from the safety of her mother's arms on the yacht's deck above. They'd made it. They were safe. She closed her eyes as relief trembled through her. Derrick's large hand skimmed along her cheek, wiping a tear from her skin.

He pressed his forehead against hers. "We're safe. It's all going to be okay."

"Okay," she whispered against his lips.

"Kiki, I—"

He crushed his mouth to hers, searing her with his need for reassurance she held in her own heart. How she wished she could stay with him forever. She wrapped her arms and legs around him, needing to be as close as possible. She wanted this memory of him to carry her through the difficult days to come. Selfish thought, just like a Payne, but she'd steal whatever moments with him she could get to keep with her when she disappeared. She wouldn't risk her family ties hurting anyone ever again.

"Finally." Rafe laughed and clapped Derrick on the back, sending a spray of water over them. "We've been taking bets on when you two would get it together."

Derrick chuckled, his fingers flexing on her waist. "You have not."

"Yep. I'm happy to say your little misadventure makes me the winner." Rafe swam backwards to the boat, a satisfied smile on his face. "I was worried I was going to have to use my impressive skills of persuasion to push you together."

Kiki tucked her head as her face heated. She couldn't let the joy settle in her heart, not when she'd be leaving the first chance she got. She pushed away from Derrick and swam to the boat.

Heart heavy, she climbed the ladder to the deck, her mind calculating possibilities. She had plans to make. Her mother would probably spend the rest of her life tucked away in some jail or something. Her depth of involvement had to be too much to get out of punishment, even if she cooperated. The rest of Kiki's family was dead, all except Eva. A lump of grief formed in Kiki's throat, for those she had lost and those she would have to let go. She had to be dead to Eva as well, in order to keep her safe.

Kiki leaned against the railing as the others made their way inside. She closed her eyes against the dropping sensation that filled her gut. Fatigue settled deep into her bones. She'd get used to the loneliness ... eventually.

"Kiki?" Zeke's voice pierced her gut with a sharp pain.

She braced herself for the recriminations sure to come.

"Thank you." Zeke's hand slid across Kiki's shoulders.

Her eyes flew open and stared at him in shock. What did he mean "thank you?"

"I don't ... I don't understand."

"You brought my baby girl home." Zeke looked out over the ocean, swallowing hard before turning his bright eyes back to Kiki. "She told me how you kept her safe and got her free."

"It's because of me they took her in the first place." Kiki rolled her shoulder, needing to get some space from the guilt.

"It could've happened with any of us." He squeezed her shoulder when she shook her head. "Yes. It could've. These terrorists knew how desperate your parents were to get Eva. If they wouldn't have gotten you, they would've still found a way to get to Eva and leverage her against Kevin to do what they wanted. It was just a matter of time."

"We should've never left the ranch with her." She huffed. "*I* should've left the ranch long ago."

"None of that kind of talk." Zeke pulled her into a

brotherly hug and led her inside. "Come on. The family's waiting."

He draped his arm across her shoulder and led her across the deck. His reaction both confused her and made her feel like she finally belonged to something bigger than herself. Too bad it couldn't last.

# THIRTY

"YOUR MOTHER HAS AGREED to cooperate for our protection." General Paxton leaned against the bar in the yacht's living room, his tone making Derrick's heart race. "Why don't you tell us what happened here, Miss Payne?"

In the hour since Derrick climbed on to the deck, he'd cleaned up, ate, given Zeke a quick rundown, and observed as Paxton and his team arrived in a flurry of questions. What Derrick hadn't done was get time to talk to Kiki, make sure she was okay. Now she stood, staring out at the ocean, telling everything that had gone down over the last three days, her tone only fluctuating when she talked of Eva. Her words left a chill to his skin. Why didn't she sit next to him? He wanted her near him, but the space between them felt as wide as the ocean beyond the windows.

"So, your aunt kidnapped you?" Rafe whistled low from where he sat sprawled on a couch. "That's messed up."

Derrick shot Rafe a glare while Sosimo whacked Rafe on the head. He was glad the team had come to help. Seeing Rafe, Sosimo, Jake, and Zeke upon approach had eased every muscle in his body that had been strung tight since the abduction. He thought he'd get to rest. He thought wrong.

"Yeah." Kiki rubbed her arm like she was cold though the room opened to the humid, tropical heat. "She ordered my brother's death." She laughed a humorless laugh. "Not really the nurturing type."

The general cleared his throat. "Marco called in. Jackie hadn't told the higher ups that Sergeant Nicholson and Eva had been brought to the complex. Said she wanted to see how she could use the information to her advantage. So Eva should be safe now that the family is gone."

"Thank God." Kiki turned to Zeke, her eyes bright with tears. "I'm so sorry."

"Kiki, we already talked about this." Zeke crossed to her from the bar and put his arm over her shoulder. It was such a big brother move, one that eased some of Derrick's worry. "None of this is your fault. You have a new life, a new family. We're just glad you all got back to us safe."

"And that you kicked terrorist butt." Rafe smiled. "Man, I wish I could've seen you take out that Edgar dope."

Her mouth twitched into an almost smile. "That was pretty satisfying."

"D, man, you got to blow up a yacht." Rafe shook his head. "I miss all the fun."

"Yeah, well, that was an accident." Derrick forced the words out of a tight throat. "I meant to disable them so the cavalry could swoop in."

"So, what now?" Jake leaned forward on the other end of the couch, his forearms resting on his legs.

"Well ... " General Paxton took a deep breath and held Kiki's gaze. "With Kiki Payne dead, we'll have to find her a new life. Young lady, we leave in ten."

The walls of the yacht's living room closed in around

Derrick even though windows covered the surface. Just what was the general playing at? Derrick's mind raced, but no words would form.

"Ay, caray." Sosimo paced behind Rafe's couch.

"We can keep her safe at the ranch. Give her new docs. No one will know it's her." Rafe scooted to the edge of the couch.

"Guys, guys." Kiki stepped away from Zeke, her hands held in front of her like she was calming a wild horse.

A stampede had just trampled Derrick. Left him bloodied and immobile.

"I can't put you all at risk. I—" Her voice cracked, and she glanced at her feet. Taking a deep breath, she peered at all of them. "I can't put Eva in danger. Thank you for showing me what a real family is."

Her gaze lingered on Derrick's, ripping his heart out of his chest. He shook his head, his movement to stand and grab her and never let go working in slow motion. Her face contorted in the misery he felt, spearing through him before she schooled it.

"General, I'm going to go say goodbye to Eva, then I'll be ready to go." She rushed from the room.

The space filled with silence, like the moment a bomb goes off at your feet. Nothing existed but the sense of emptiness and the screaming agony of his heart. He couldn't lose her. Couldn't handle never seeing her again.

He clenched his jaw, his eyes connecting with Zeke's. With a sad smile and a nod toward Kiki, Zeke turned to the general. Derrick shot to his feet and raced from the room.

As he hotfooted it, Zeke's words pushed Derrick on. "General, I have an idea."

Derrick dashed down the stairs, taking them by threes. Rounding the corner, Kiki leaned against the wall, stopping him short. Her hands covered her face and shoulders shook in silent sobs.

"Kiki."

She jerked her head up, quickly wiping her face. She shook her head and stepped down the hall.

"Derrick, please. I need to see Eva."

He sprinted down the hall, grabbed her elbow, and pulled her to a stop. Relief coursed through him when she didn't struggle. Then despair flooded the relief away as she peered up at him with determination blazing in her beautiful, clear blue eyes.

"I'm not letting you go." Derrick took her other arm.

She lifted her hands and gripped his biceps. "You have to. I can't stay, Derrick. I ... I won't put the others at risk like that." Her hold on him tightened. "Please, please understand. Y'all are the only family I've ever really had. I love you." She shook her head, her actions contradicting her declaration. "I love all of you. The organization knows I lived there. If it surfaces that my mother survived somehow during the investigation or case, the organization will assume I lived too. Even if we change my name, they know what I look like. They'll come looking at the ranch."

No, he wouldn't accept that. He closed his eyes, frustration welling up inside him. She was right. She'd analyzed all the data and picked the only option that would pay out. He wrapped his arms around her.

"I can't lose you." His words tumbled through the sharp shards closing his throat.

She leaned her forehead on his chest, her fingers tangling in his shirt. "I ... I can't stay."

"Then I'm coming with you." Purpose burned hot in his gut.

"No." She pushed off of him, but he held tight. "No,

Derrick. You'll lose everything. Not just Stryker, but your family. I can't let you do that."

"Honey, I only lose everything if I lose you."

Hope flashed in her eyes before distress chased it away. "With Kiki Payne dead, I won't have anything. We won't have anything. And you'd never be able to contact your friends, your parents." She pushed harder as her voice rose and tears streamed down her face. "I'm not worth you giving all that up."

"Shh, honey, listen." He cupped her face in his hands and kissed her softly on the lips. "I don't care if they put us in a one-room cabin in the Alaskan wilderness. I love you. My family will understand."

He touched his lips to hers. They tasted of salty tears, of the future. She sobbed, throwing her arms around him and kissing him hard in return. Was she agreeing or saying good-bye? It didn't matter. He'd follow her to the ends of the world until she understood he wasn't giving up on them. She pulled away, her chin trembling as she stared into his eyes.

"I'm coming." He rubbed his thumb over her cheek to brush away the tears.

She held his gaze, her chest rising and falling in an exaggerated breath. "Okay."

Joy exploded into his chest and made his knees loose. Life shifted back into place. The details of that life didn't matter as long as she remained in his arms.

"I have a better idea than you two disappearing off the face of the planet." Zeke's amused voice punctured the bubble where only Kiki existed.

Derrick tucked her under his arm, as close to his body as he could. "Yeah? What's that?"

"I've been wanting to set up safe houses, like the island, but manned, hiding as businesses of their own." Zeke sauntered down the hall like he had all the time in the world. Could he just get to the point? A conspiring smile turned his lips up. "How does a ranch in Montana sound?"

Derrick's forehead crinkled, then smoothed as what Zeke implied took root. Could they make it work, keeping Kiki safely hidden? Derrick trusted his team could do whatever was needed. How could he be getting everything he'd dreamed of and not lose a thing?

Zeke clapped Derrick on the shoulder. "We'll get busy making you two disappear."

"What ... what just happened?" Kiki leaned her head back to look up at him.

"I believe we have a way to stay underground but not lose it all." He pulled her into a full embrace. "This means we'll have to marry, get new names, and move to Montana, but we should still be able to see the others for visits."

Kiki stifled a smile. "Is that your way of proposing?"

He slid his hands up her back and threaded his fingers through her hair. Her sassy attitude and the hope of what their life would be filled him until he thought he'd float away. His heart beat so hard in his chest he was sure she could feel it.

"Kiki, I love you. I know all of this is happening fast and that your life will change forever." He kissed her once on her soft lips. "But I'd like that change to be with me firmly by your side."

"I love you too." Emotion choked her whisper, but she wrapped her arms around his neck and crashed her mouth to his.

As he dived into her, everything else disappeared. The

future may be a little fuzzy. So many details needed hammering out. Life could be in utter chaos, but as long as that life was with her, it didn't matter.

# EPILOGUE

KIKI LEANED against the rough fence and scanned the open meadow where horses chomped the sweet Montana grass. While the towering mountain view, the scent of pine and wildflowers, and the cool breeze resembled the Stryker ranch back in Colorado, her life was anything but the same. The last month had settled from the buzz of frantic actions needed to scrub a life clean and start over. New home, new job, and a new name in the span of a handful of days.

Well, the last she didn't mind at all. Her lips twitched up as warmth filled her core. Being Kirsten Hunter, wife to David Hunter, wasn't so bad. In fact, she had never felt more herself than she did in her new life. When Derrick had said he wanted to take the last name Hunter after the special ops friend that had disappeared while camping, Kiki's heart had melted just a bit. Picking David, because they could conquer giants together, liquified it to a puddle of mush. How her life had turned from ash to blessed still overwhelmed her.

Heat enveloped her as Derrick's arms boxed her in. She

leaned back against him, letting the sense of safety and love fill her. He traced kisses along her shoulder to that sensitive spot behind her ear, fanning the embers that always smoldered just beneath the surface. A horse whinnied and dashed to the fence. Kiki's heart skipped as Derrick groaned into her neck.

"I think she's jealous." Kiki snickered, elbowing him lightly in the gut.

"Yeah, I think you're right." He pulled her closer, leaning his chin on her head as the brown mare rushed to greet her favorite person.

Derrick had worried that moving the two mares so soon after rescuing them would make them jumpier, but since arriving at their new place, the brown mare had blossomed. The palomino had relaxed as well, coming to Kiki occasionally for a treat.

"Hey, Reeses." Derrick chuckled as the mare pushed her head over the fence and up against Derrick's. "Missed me, did ya?"

Kiki still chuckled at the names Eva had chosen for the two horses. Reeses and Payday, after two of her favorite candies. Though all candy seemed to be Eva's favorite.

"Okay, enough." Derrick patted the mare on the neck and threaded his fingers through Kiki's, leading her back to the large ranch house. "Well, wife, it looks like everything worked out just like we planned. The Redemption Ranch is all set up as a horse rescue and rehabilitation center. Rafe's buried us so deep, no one will ever connect our ranch here to Stryker Security."

"And we're all set as a safe house if they need it for clients?" Kiki wrapped her arm around Derrick's waist, hooking her fingers in his belt loop.

"Yeah." He sighed. "There are still additions we'll want to make so the ranch is even safer, but it'll work exactly how Zeke envisioned."

She loved being close beside him. Loved how he always found a reason to touch her. Cherished how they'd found peace and comfort so different from the busyness they'd left in Colorado. She had worried he'd regret leaving the excitement and camaraderie Stryker provided, but each day he seemed to lose himself more and more in life on their ranch. A weight he'd hidden so well had lifted from his shoulders, leaving a man quick to laugh and shrug off the many changes in plans necessary to pull off setting up their life.

"When is your video chat with the ladies?" Derrick's voice rumbled huskily.

"In two hours. They're going to call at the wedding dress shop so I can help pick out Chloe's gown." If there was anything she missed, it was having the girls around, but being able to talk was a blessing she hadn't imagined she'd have. "Even Lena is going to be there."

"Hmm. That's gonna be rough on her. Ever since Ethan died, she's avoided anything wedding related like the plague." Derrick's thoughtfulness always hit Kiki hard. Maybe because it was such a contrast to Kiki's own family.

"So ... " Not wanting to slide down the slope thoughts of her family brought, she squeezed him closer. "What's on the agenda today?"

"Well, we've got the house to ourselves." He stopped and pulled her flush against him.

"We always have the house to ourselves." She chuckled.

"I think we can find a way to occupy the next two hours. Maybe some slow dancing." He wagged his eyebrows up and down.

Kiki's head fell back as a joyful laugh pushed forth. In a swift move, he swept her up into his arms and rushed up the porch stairs. Life had turned out far from what she ever imagined, but Derrick's love convinced her it was more than worth it.

## SNEAK PEEK - HONORING LENA

LENA REBEL'S skin itched as another round of giggles erupted between her friends. She glanced at her watch and inwardly groaned. They'd been at the dress shop for only thirty minutes, which meant Lena had at least two hours of torture left.

Not that she didn't want to be with Chloe, Piper, Sam, and June. Even Cookie had made it via video, blushing every time someone mentioned Derrick. Being on this extended assignment, pretending to be nanny to ex-Congressman Marshall Rand's son, had shown her how thankful Lena was for the Stryker team and being brought into that odd family. She could've gone home to Alaska, but the dreams she and Ethan had built, dreams of running a guiding business side-by-side, haunted her with heart-wrenching sorrow every time she went home.

She knew it wasn't good to still mourn so deeply over losing her chance at being Mrs. Ethan Stryker. Yet the anger surrounding his death kept the hurt boiling, scorching her with every thought of him. It was fine, really. She'd rather live with the pain than risk her heart again.

Besides, she wasn't the only one that held onto mourning, refusing to let it slip through their fingers. Marshall Rand's dark blue eyes that reminded Lena of a troubled sea flashed in her mind. Losing his wife still burdened him, though he seemed better equipped to hide it than Lena. Strange how the death of his wife encouraged him to vote for the bill that caused Ethan's demise.

Lena wanted to hate Marshall. Yet the longer she protected his son, the more her thoughts inched toward respect. The increase of her pulse flushed her skin with anger. It didn't matter what the man did now. Him flipping his support of the bill two years before killed Ethan—her fiancé. The only one who'd seen through the tough, awkward girl to the woman within.

Sam glanced at Lena from where the ladies aahed over Chloe's latest gown, a look of concern on her face. Lena forced a smile and stomped to the buffet of finger foods set out. She'd protect Mr. Rand's son with her life if she had to. However, she wouldn't ... couldn't allow anything but disdain to surface for the man who had destroyed her dreams.

## ALSO BY SARA BLACKARD

*Want to know what happened the first time Derrick was at that Colombian Complex? Mission Out of Control is the FREE prequel short story of the mission that went terribly wrong.*

It was a mission like any other ... until it blew apart around them.

When the Army's Special Ops team is tasked with infiltrating the Columbian jungle and rescuing a kidnapped State Department family, the mission seems like every other one they've executed. But as the assignment unravels, not only is the mission's success at stake, but all the brothers-in-arms leaving the jungle alive hangs in the balance.

www.sarablackard.com

## ABOUT THE AUTHOR

Sara Blackard has been a writer since she was able to hold a pencil. When she's not crafting wild adventures and sweet romances, she's homeschooling her five children, keeping their off-grid house running, or enjoying the Alaskan lifestyle she and her husband love.

Made in the USA
Las Vegas, NV
20 April 2021